REBECCA O'ROURKE was born in Manchester in 1955. After a convent education which she describes as having survived 'relatively unscathed', she went to Hull University where she encountered the Women's and Gay Liberation Movements. She continued her research into women's writing at the Centre for Contemporary Cultural Studies in Birmingham. A teacher in adult education for several years, she has always been interested in the history of working-class writing, particularly in the contribution of women to it. In 1978 she became involved with the Federation of Worker Writers and Community Publishers and through that involvement began to draw together the different strands in her own life and gained the confidence to write about them. She has contributed to a number of anthologies, amongst them *Where There's Smoke* and *The Likes of Us*, as well as co-authoring two works of non-fiction, *The Republic of Letters* and *Re-writing English*.

Rebecca O'Rourke lives in north London and works at Centerprise in Hackney, a community publisher and bookshop which publishes and promotes working-class writers.

In *Jumping the Cracks*, Rebecca O'Rourke's first novel, young lesbian Rats experiences the city in all its menace after finding a dead body dumped in a Rolls on a -dark Hackney street. Despite the complications of a job in a seedy accommodation agency teetering on the edge of legality, and an erratic relationship with her lover Helen, Rats won't be diverted from her obsessive attempts to track down the killer. Politics and crime, love and loneliness, the search for origins and understanding, combine together to create an exciting thriller and an evocative picture of modern urban life.

JUMPING
THE
CRACKS

Rebecca O'Rourke

VIRAGO

Published by VIRAGO PRESS Limited 1987
41 William IV Street, London WC2N 4DB

British Library Cataloguing in Publication Data

O'Rourke, Rebecca
   Jumping the cracks.
   I. Title
   823'.914 [F]   PR6065.R69/

   ISBN 0-86068-767-8
   ISBN 0-86068-771-6 Pbk

Printed in Great Britain by
Anchor Brendon of Tiptree, Essex

Acknowledgements

The writing of this book and its publication entails many debts. Years before this book emerged is the debt of writing itself: the encouragement, excitement and challenge of the Federation of Worker Writers and Community Publishers. This particular novel owes a great deal to the enthusiasm of Hackney Women Writers' Workshop, particularly Margaret Quigley and, like all my writing, it was enjoyed, criticised and developed there and in Hackney Writers' Workshop.

Being published is all together different from writing. Pluto Press announced their Crime Novel competition some months after I started *Jumping the Cracks* and being shortlisted, having my writing appreciated and recognised publicly was an enormous boost to my confidence. Jenny Uglow has my great thanks for helping me approach a publisher and sustaining my confidence while doing that. Ruthie Petrie, my editor at Virago, has been patient, rigorous and caring: everything a first-time author could want.

The process of re-writing, much harder than the initial excitement and pleasure of writing the book, has been eased by many people. I appreciate their interest, time, encouragement and willingness to help me improve my writing, both for this and future works. The people I work with at Centerprise have tolerated my obsession with writing, especially when it comes into conflict with doing my job.

Throughout this time I have been sustained and inspired by the generosity, patience and kindness of Jean Milloy. She has my greatest thanks.

For Jane, and for Jean

1

It began on a wet, windy night in Hackney. The cover had worked loose on one of the street lights towering above the roadway stretching down towards Dalston. The wind rocked it back and forth, casting slabs of light across the pavement. It looked as if some huge figure were swinging a flashlight at random, illuminating, momentarily, the nooks and crannies of a street declining into dereliction.

It was nearly midnight and as she approached the junction it suddenly went dark. The creaking of the lamp dominated the empty street. Speeding up her pace, Rats crossed the street just as the lights came back on. She walked along the building site hoardings and turned into Caitlin Road. Three out of four of its street lights were out. The dim yellow glow of the sole survivor lit the usual scenes: lights dimmed in The Bronx and the knot of people just inside its door, the smell of fried chicken floating above the stale diesel street smells; empty orange milk crates outside Patel's, the grocer's.

Cars were doubled parked to the brow of the incline marking the bridge over the railway line. As Rats walked up the street, scraps of litter, caught by the wind, were trapped in the heavy thud of her feet one after another along the pavement. She tried to kick away a plastic food bag and, slipping on its shiny surface, came to an unsteady halt – Rats was drunk – it seemed to be taking a long time to get home tonight and battling with the wind and rubbish underfoot wasn't helping. She noticed the car before she came level with it. She'd seen it around a lot. Mostly parked outside the garage near the lime-green community cafe, a kind of drop-in place for down-and-outs, people with time to kill. The Rolls Royce looked smooth and tasteful, its dark, mellow green standing out against the grimy streets. As Rats drew close to it she saw that it was parked at a slight angle to the pavement.

Perhaps that was why she paused, and peered in. As a rule, cars like that have an invisible shield. To go closer is to trespass, invade the life that drives a car like that. She had stepped up close to cars like these as a teenager when, in gangs of three or four, she and her friends would roam through the city centre after nightfall and deliberately run

1

penknives and coins across the paintwork of cars clearly bigger and better, newer and shinier than those they grew up around.

Having paused, it was easy to stop and having stopped to see the door was slightly open. Some curiosity made her lean forward almost into the car, perhaps a momentary urge to take the car and drive off, even though she couldn't drive. Later, she was to forget there had ever been that moment of choice, that it had been as possible not to look as to look, not to stop as to stop.

It was as if she simply and suddenly was alongside, seeing that there was somebody in the passenger seat, half out of the seat, propping the door ajar. Her attention caught by the unnatural attitude, Rats slowly realised why it slumped the way it did. Blood was congealing on the back of the seat, a dark chilling stain. The skull had a ragged split. This was no longer a person, but a corpse, mirroring back her own shock in its gaping mouth and startled staring eyes.

She stood stock still and looked. As the gorge rose in her throat she turned aside, found herself opening the door of a phone box, further back down the street. She stood there. The stale smell of the phone box mixed with the fresher stench of piss. She stood, her nostrils assailed, heart pounding, her stomach heaving. She thought she should phone an ambulance. A man had died out there. She thought to call the police but something stopped her. You don't call the police lightly in Hackney, not with their history of beatings, even deaths, to extort confessions; accidental deaths because their cars go too fast, for no good reason.

All her life, the police had been on the wrong side, the other side. From when they stopped her and her friends during the summer evenings of their childhoods for no other reason than they were out on the streets in noisy gangs, to the regular visits searching for the stolen property they assumed went hand in hand with working on the docks, as her father had done. She couldn't phone the police but she had to phone an ambulance. As she picked up the receiver there was no note. The line was dead. She could phone no one.

She stood there, scared and trapped by the phone box with its promise of contact, help, other people, and as the silence resounded in her head, it seemed to ring out in the dark, wet street, saying there is no contact, no relief. There are only panes of glass, little enough between you and the dark, wild street with its lives behind shaded windows, its closed doors and the body, up the road, its life drained out onto the rutted broken pavement.

2

She was suddenly nine years old, followed home by a drunken groping, leering man whose steps were heavier, whose strides were longer than her own. He almost caught her, drew level and touched her. She ran in blind panic, along Shaw Heath to reach the phone box. Fell inside, picked up the receiver, fingers finding 999. The connection was dead and the man opened the door. Some presence of mind led her to begin talking, describing the man, the situation and where they were. The door closed and he lurched beerily away. Then, as now, she had stood drawing her breath with a strong sense of pleasure in its very existence. Scared she might be, adrenalin racing through her body, making her heart beat wildly, her hands tremble and drying her mouth, but she was there. She could not stay indefinitely in the phone box. She would have to walk back past the car, past the body. She would have to decide what to do. She pushed against the door with her shoulder and slipped out into the night. She began to walk up the familiar pavement, words from long forgotten pop songs running, irrelevantly, through her head. She was less than ten minutes away from home. She continued to walk, drew level with the car and walked past it.

As she quickened her pace she was overcome with a sense of panic. Whoever, whatever had produced this mess of blood and body back there in the sleek confines of a well-upholstered car could still be about. The eyes that followed the path of that axe or bullet could be watching her, assessing the vulnerability of her broad back in its leather jacket. Taking its aim on the nape of her neck, taking account of the rise and fall of her body as it moved out of, and into, range. She felt sweat trickling down between her shirt and flesh. She had no choice but to keep walking, could not run, could not admit panic. Sober now, her only hope was to walk, conscious of the ludicrous prospect of an anonymous death on these streets. Her talisman, her desire to reach home, was strong enough to carry her on past the trees that could hide the killer, the houses that stood as silent witnesses, to her own front door.

Reaching its familiar steps, she dragged herself up them, her legs weakening, her trembling hands threatening to drop the keys, obstruct her passage into its relative safety and security. But she was there. She was switching the light on, weaving her way around her cat as he danced her to the kitchen and his feeding bowls, plugging in the heater. She spooned cat-food into his bowl, emptied the milk into a china bowl patterned with blue cornflowers, unscrewed the whiskey

3

bottle. Eventually she slept, where she sat. Dressed, ready for flight, the glass overturned on the floor beside her.

2

Dawn broke over London as it breaks over any city. The first exodus of people to work happens by half light, cold and frosty. They mingle, interchangeable with people going home from night shift. The sleepy irritability of the bus conductor could be that of a man going home after a hard night, or a woman, dragging herself from her sleep-warm bed to run the early morning service, just one step ahead of her passengers. Large parts of a city like London never sleep, they change their rhythms and patterns to fit the ebb and flow of activity around them. Emergency switchboards, casualty departments, sewerage pumping stations, all night garages. Machines ticking and humming, lights flashing on and off in sequence, a rhythm overseen, intervened into, by people. So many, they become a mass. Undifferentiated, simply working. Whether they pour tea into a cafe's chipped mug and tend the toasting machine or pick up the steaming mug, people meet across the simple facts of living, producing warmth, exchanges of conversation, the rub and bustle of a city moving into gear.

In Stoke Newington, work was underway. The lights of the Primary School, left on all night to warn off intruders, were beginning to look out of place as they shone into the dawn breaking over Caitlin Road. The light swept round and into the room where Rats slumped in a chair, was sleeping awkwardly. A blank, dark space broken by fragments of conversations, half remembered faces, moments of insight marked by nothing more significant than the shifting of her body in search of a comfortable position, the slide of her cat dropping from lap to floor.

She started awake, unsure where she was, what she saw. Her room, simple in its cluttered untidiness, faded into the sleek lines of an expensive car and the ragged intrusions of the body. She had been dreaming, the empty bottle that she would be hard put to replace

4

rolled across the threadbare carpet as she stretched her legs out. Why had she drunk all that whiskey? Remembering, a wave of nausea gripped her. She staggered to the toilet, her head beating with the sick, throbbing pain of a hangover. She threw up a night of booze, greasy food, the memory of the body. Jerked with the spasms of vomiting, her head seemed unsteadily her own. Slowly, as the thin morning light thickened into weak sunlight, she undressed, showered and got herself to bed. Aspirin for the pain, water for the dehydration. She needed to sleep it off.

Too frequently, these last few months, Rats had been putting herself to bed like this. Caring for herself showed only as the ability to manage her hangovers. She wouldn't admit questions of why she had them, why she needed to drink herself into a stupor on the nights her dole cheque held out. She had been unlucky in love. A common enough predicament.

The magazines said find yourself another man, cultivate your friends, take up a hobby. They all assumed that some day, somewhere, Mr Right was waiting in the wings with his 2.5 children, his mortgage on a pleasant home, his reliable firm's car. The magazines had every answer to every variant of man trouble. They didn't have a lot to offer if your trouble was woman trouble. She pulled herself into a heap on the left hand side of the bed.

She woke again just after noon. It wasn't signing-on day, it wasn't a giro day. It wasn't even a day to spend down at the benefit office trying to unravel the intricacies of receiving the benefit to which she was entitled on time and in full. It was a formless, empty day, half over before it began. Friends of hers still working envied this time, considered she wasted it. If they were her, they nagged her, they'd go swimming at least twice a week, sign up for classes at the local centre, learn a new language, take up a hobby. Make some changes, get involved. Rats knew exactly what they'd do. She'd done it herself for the first three or four months after she'd lost her job. But gradually, her resilience had worn down. She'd been working, on and off, for the last twelve years. She had grown used to work even if she hadn't liked it.

As Rats woke up, the memory of her walk home came back into focus. With a start she remembered it, not as the nightmare she thought it could have been, but real. Seen with her own eyes. Eyes she now closed, trying to get the images out of her sight. She lay there trembling with the shock, forcing herself to stop thinking about it, trying to forget. She couldn't. She tried to anchor herself somewhere and found a kind of comfort in the old worry of her unemployment. She would have to find a job. The rooms she lived in were rented through an agency, the landlord just a name on a form she'd signed over a year ago. She had been working when she took the place, the agency had insisted on that. They hadn't been informed when she lost her job, but must have noticed how some weeks the rent arrived late or not at all. She was nearly a month in arrears, a critical period. The agents held a month's rent in lieu of damage or debt. When that ran out they would begin to lose money. Already they had sent one threatening letter. And the other tenants in the house, sensitive as they were to the ebb and flow of life in there, must have noticed that she was around during the day, had ceased to run her life to the rhythm of regular work.

Thinking about the need to find work had a sharper edge today. The scene last night intruded. Rats went over it again, remembering how drunk she had been, wondering if she could have imagined it. The shock was real, the vivid detail of the death. It unnerved her, the realisation that life could end suddenly and messily on a street in a run down part of town. What would there be left to call her life if it had been her?

Rats needed to work. She shivered against the morbid pull of that man's death and the power it gave her own life. All sorts of reasons now made work urgent. And most practical of all was the need for money in her pocket and a place to live. She knew how hard it was finding a place in London, even in the unfashionable poorer parts. And being there she had no choices about being anywhere else.

She got up, made coffee, took it back to bed. Lying there, with the radio's endless messages about events in the public world, she sipped her coffee, stroked her cat and made decisions. She would get up, get dressed, go out and buy a paper. She would call by the job centre. She was ready to do almost anything. Rats was trained to work as a typist. Way back, it had seemed like a good idea, a route to better jobs, regular money and a sense of achievement. It wasn't factory work or shop work. It amused her, sometimes, to think what a great step up in the world her sixty words per minute had once seemed.

She hadn't stayed in any job for long, had never been able to stand the office gossip, the questions about what you did with who; engagement, pregnancy, marriage. In her early years Rats hadn't gone out much, had no boyfriend. If she'd done good works or had a sympathetic ear, been somehow old before her time, she might have got by as a surrogate aunt to the office. But she hadn't. She had simply been awkward, unlike the others, but different too from the temps, the students, women clear about what they were doing in offices: earning money, putting up with things. Rats was puzzled: it should have been a good life and it wasn't. She went from job to job, office to office in the years when it was still possible.

Gradually, painfully, she had begun to sort out her differences with the rest of the women, her family and her friends. It had lost her jobs, references, friends and finally, her family. Sometimes it seemed to Rats that she had lost the world for Helen. When she lost Helen, it was like the lights going out for good, waking up one day to find everyone speaking a language she didn't understand. She hadn't been able to talk to anyone about it. The limits of their small town, hidden lives had never seemed so tightly drawn. That's why she came to London. That's why . . . she stopped the train of thought. She knew where it ended too well. Today was different, right. Pity the poor bastard who'd set it up for you, yes, but no pity for yourself. Nothing. Things are final in this world. As final as the blood smeared across the leather seat of that expensive car. The memory took hold of her, but she pushed it away. It had been bad but the shock had worked, kicked her out of her rut, leaving a residue of fear, making her jumpy. She had to move, try and face it down.

When she hit the street she toyed with the idea of taking another route. She was reluctant to go back to the scene, apprehensive as to what she would find. The police would be long gone. Not everyone would have been as squeamish as her about calling them, or the inevitable patrol car would have found its excuse for the wailing sirens that played their melodies through the hours of darkness. She took her usual route.

As she approached the bottom of the street, her heart began to tickle her ribs, hiccuping inside her shirt. But there was no cause for alarm. No shadow loomed lightly, restraining her with the words 'Madam, if you would . . . a person answering your description was . . .' We police ourselves she thought, excusing and explaining her behaviour in her head.

There was nothing unusual there. A van unloading, the knot of women with pushchairs and children outside the playgroup; Marmalade from the launderette stretching up against the plywood furniture stacked outside the DIY store. Patel's crates now covered with plastic turf, boxes of fruits and vegetables laid out on top. The Bronx was closed up for the day, several stacked black plastic bags on the pavement in front. There was no cordoned off area; no thin chalk lines. Nothing to mark the passage of violent death. It was a normal, everyday scene with people going about their business as if nothing unusual had happened in the dark. Two worlds, in an area like this, the day and the night. No exchanges, just people like herself passing uneasily between them.

The same scraps of paper hung to the gutter, the same leaves were being trampled into the rub and grime of the street. But the car and the body had been cleansed, leaving no traces in the sticky rush of matter down the drain.

And people come and go as easily. The no-hopers down on their luck, young boys and girls drawn by the bright lights of the capital fall into its shadows as quietly and easily. Packaged in plastic bags, labelled with their names, if known, a description if not, to wait in mortuaries and funeral parlours. You get your dustbin emptied less regularly than this city clears away its dead.

Rats was as disturbed by the swift disappearance of the body as its sudden entrance into her life. Its absence didn't relieve her fear. She almost wanted it there. Something tangible to hold against the universe, out of place as it seemed in the bustling street. Scraps of conversation brought her back to herself.

She crossed the road, bought a *Hackney Gazette* and went into the Empress Cafe. The bed and breakfast families from up the road were drifting in to spend their lunch allowance on cups of tea. She found it painful to meet the eyes of these women, beaten down by lack of money, saddled with out-of-work husbands. They eyed the fruit machine as if it held some kind of hope for them. She needn't have worried about meeting their eyes: they kept them low. Pulled their thin coats around them, wiped the noses of their kids and kept an eye to their husbands as they sat across from them, layering tomato sauce and salad cream on to slices of bread.

Rats drank her tea and ate her food, turning the paper to the classified section. There wasn't a lot on offer. She scribbled down any phone numbers that held promise, checked her store of loose change and finished her tea. As she left the cafe the woman from the table next to hers reached for Rats' untouched second piece of toast. Their eyes met in a reproachful gaze: the woman's need, her waste. She let the door swing to, coming up against the musky smells of the chrysanthemums and hyacinths in pots outside the flower shop. She had turned back towards Caitlin Road before she remembered the phones weren't working. As she made her way over to the Church Street, she wondered how she could forget.

The first three jobs she called had just gone. The fourth didn't answer. The fifth asked her to come for an interview, at 2.30. It was over on Mare Street. She walked up the High Street, aware of the buzz and flow of traffic.

The red diesel buses pulled across the road like it was a race track. On the pavement she moved solidly against the crush, past a pensioner spinning out her shopping, talking to a bored stall holder; past the young people idling around the record shop. She joined the people like herself, trying to pretend they had some reason to be moving purposefully down the street. The people with jobs were already at them, locked into their clock cards and time sheets. The rest were just kidding themselves.

Anxious about being late she got on a bus from Dalston Junction to Mare Street and found herself outside Lindy Property Agents with five minutes to spare and five minutes to be early. She read through the cards in the window. They all offered a roof over your head: one, two or three bedrooms, kitchen shared, rate and rent inclusive for about £30 per week. No fees to landlords, fancy hand-written signs and a neon light for when the office was shut. Style and glitter on the backs of people with no style and no glitter. Rats heard the little bell tinkle as she pushed the door open and stepped inside. 'Hello,' she said, 'I've come about the job. I rang earlier, my name's Gerry Flannagan.'

A middle-aged man looked up at her. He said, 'Wait here, would you,' then moved out of the office into the back. A few minutes later he emerged with a younger woman.

'Maureen'll show you around, won't you, love?'
His arm lingered on her waist as he brought her through to the room. She wore heels that seemed to Rats too high for safety or comfort and a knitted red dress. It stretched over her full breasts and slightly bulging stomach. She was made up, just a fraction too heavily for the time and place. Her collection of bangles jangled as she moved. Taking Rats in with a glance, half pitying, half amused, she asked, 'Have you experience of this kind of work?'

'Not exactly.' Christ, she thought, not the way to talk yourself into a job.

9

'I mean, I've done lots of clerical work before: my shorthand and typing are good and I've done reception work before, for a dentist's so it's not that relevant.'

Maureen and the man smiled at each other.

'It can get painful in here sometimes you know,' the man said, 'people not paying their rent, that sort of thing. I reckon if you kept your head in a dentist's waiting room you can manage this place.' They both laughed at this.

'Don't listen to him, love, I don't.'

Rats stood and watched, waiting for them to calm down. It was a long time since she'd seen people behaving this way, like kids they were, with some great secret. She smiled at Maureen.

'Come on round and let me see your typing. Here, copy this letter and honest, love, don't take him seriously, right. You might end up like me.'

Rats sat at the typewriter, put a piece of carbon between a top sheet of headed paper and flimsy.

'Do you make one or two copies?'

'Just the one.'

She typed the letter. It was easy. She'd spent years of her life spacing out the messages of business life; correcting spelling mistakes and grammar as unobtrusively as she knew. It was a simple matter to sit and type out a two paragraph letter.

Maureen came and looked it over. 'Great,' she said, 'This job is probably only going to be temporary, is that okay?'

'Sure how long?'

'I'm having a baby.'

This set them off again and was obviously the cause of the merriment.

'And we are married. But it's my first and I'm not as young as I used to be, so Ralph and I aren't taking any chances. I'm stopping work just as soon as I can and I won't be straight back after it's born. Does that bother you? We'd give you proper notice but we can't guarantee anything.'

Rats said it sounded fine. Then Maureen ran through the rest of her duties. They sounded pretty straightforward. Letters to tenants, prospective tenants, landlords and would-be landlords. Keeping files up to date and checking who had paid rent and who hadn't, reminders and receipts. Ralph did the banking and the books. He selected the clients, landlords and tenants. She might have to show the odd tenant around a new flat but she didn't make any decisions. She also made the coffee, bought the stamps and cleaned the office every morning before it opened. They were paying £70 a week. She was to start the following week.

She'd liked them. She hadn't liked their business, it was as parasitical as you could get. People always needed a place to live. She'd been to agencies herself. But these people were okay. The office was chaotic and bubbling. That was probably Maureen; vibrant, a good woman to work with. Ralph had been all over her, hands everywhere. Rats wondered how he'd manage with her gone, whether his hands were permanently in search of warm female flesh. Probably, that sort usually were. Still, she knew what to do. She reckoned Maureen did too. Just one word. She'd threaten him and then she'd do it, tell Maureen. She had no compunction about men like Ralph.

As Rats walked back it struck her that she was working very hard on liking these people. There was no reason to like them, no reason to feel as grateful as she did. It was just a job. But the sun was starting to set, the sky turned crimson and Rats felt the whole city hold itself in like a breath. It is something, it is something, she muttered to herself. It's a start. Don't deny yourself that.

And why deny people their happiness? Okay, so they're running a business like a scab on a sick body: but is that their fault? They needn't have taken her on. She felt elated. Decided to go down the club that evening. Just to sit and drink a few beers and watch the women there, in twos and threes. Smile at the others, like herself, there on their own. Maybe accept a dance or two, maybe take the initiative. And afterwards, she would come up the basement steps and out into the night air of Essex Road to the 73 bus and home to bed alone. You had to take things in stages.

On the way home she bought a *Standard*. I need to know your name, mate, just to say thank you. To know who to drink to tonight. She felt sick as she tried to read, buses always made her feel like that. So she rolled the paper up and tapped it against the seat in front. As she approached the street she felt her stomach lurch, a sense of panic hit her. It was getting dark now, shadowy late afternoon darkness, but the scene was not so different from that she'd seen earlier in the day when light had filtered out the ghosts and shadows. There were people going about their daily lives, unconcerned and untroubled. She walked on and became part of them. Coming into the flat she went straight into the kitchen to feed the cat. Then she took her coat off and lay on her bed.

11

She read the paper from cover to cover. No mention of him. He hadn't even made it to the *Standard*, poor bastard. She'd probably never know who he was now. But it was behind her, and now her life had a structure again. Her passport back to the official world. The world of grown-up people with responsibilities and commitments, demands on their time, pay packets to look forward to. She took a shower and dressed in entirely clean clothes, even clean knickers. She hummed softly, tunelessly. You never know, she thought, you never know – until her mother's voice intruded on her fantasy of where she might spend the night, 'Yer want clean pants on if you're going out, girl. Yer might get run over!'

3

Rats missed having someone to share her news with, missed Helen if she were honest with herself. Since being in London she had made some friends, had a few casual affairs, but nothing came near the ease and excitement she had known with Helen. Once she became unemployed her social life dwindled away, Brenda was the only friend she saw regularly and she was working away until Easter.

The idea that Monday morning was worth looking forward to made her smile. All the times in her life she'd never wanted Sunday to end. But this Sunday it had been a pleasure to wash her clothes and clean her shoes for work. It was a delight to set her alarm before she got into bed.

Come the morning she was up before she needed to be, dressed and setting out for work early. She arrived to find the building closed. For a moment she thought she might have invented the job, invented Lindy's Property Agents. But the neon sign shining above the shop front was solid enough and, as she waited, the prospect of work was real. A Ford Cortina drew up, a woman emerged, ungainly.

'Didn't he give you a key? Hang on, love, he's just parking.' Maureen lumbered up to her. She seemed suddenly more pregnant than Rats remembered, her stomach carrying all before her. She bent down to the shutter, then stood up, her hand on her back and handed Rats the keys.

'Open up for us, love, I can't manage it.'

Rats unlocked the door and pushed it open. Maureen followed her in. While Rats stood, awkward as a customer, Maureen had switched on the lights, a heater and was filling the kettle.

'I'll get a cuppa on, can't start the day without one,' she said.

Rats picked up the bundle of mail from the floor and put it on the desk.

'I'll be glad to stop this lark. I'm done for and we haven't started yet.' Maureen was setting out mugs, sniffing the milk cartons and discarding them, searching in her bag for fresh.

'Do you take sugar?'

There were three mugs of tea on the counter as Ralph came through the door. He picked up one of the mugs and disappeared into the back. Maureen took a few sips of her tea, added another spoonful of sugar and leaned up against the counter.

'Ready when you are,' said Rats.

Rats' first impressions of Maureen were confirmed as the morning wore on and they worked together. Ralph spent the morning in the back room, apart from the three trips he made to ask whether they were brewing up. The work seemed straightforward, a combination of secretarial and reception work with some basic book-keeping and, it seemed to Rats, more servicing of Ralph than was strictly fair.

Lindy's was a combined accommodation agency and property management service. They also arranged insurance for those properties they managed. Maureen outlined the day-to-day office routines. The buying of stamps, filing, dealing with the post, operating a petty cash float, entering in the cash and day books rents collected and requested, maintaining customer and client accounts, answering phone queries.

'It's organisation really. If you're organised it's straightforward, quite a pleasant job. Very little unpleasantness,' said Maureen.

'There is some then? How come?'

Maureen looked at her nails, studied them intently, then picked up the reception book as if moving on. Rats continued to look at her, smiling. 'What d'ye mean?' she said.

Maureen looked at the back room, then at Rats. When she spoke her voice was quieter. 'I don't think it'll affect you. It's him really. You know how it is, people can be funny about houses, unreasonable sometimes I think. They come round, argue with him. I don't understand what it's about. Probably he'll just send you home. I always had to wait for him so I'd hear them shouting and carrying on through there, and some of them were pretty rude to me when they left. But don't worry about it. It doesn't happen that often. And anyway, these things blow over.'

This explanation satisfied Rats, she had no desire to dwell on it. They moved on to the other side of her job, dealing with the public. Maureen explained that most of their accommodation clients came in off the street. They didn't advertise, they didn't need to. 'There's always people looking for a place to live,' she said. 'It'd be a waste of our money.'

Their services as property managers were, however, quite heavily advertised. A few of their houses were owned privately, left to a son or daughter who didn't want to live in them or sell. The bulk of the property they managed was owned by various companies. Of these, Magnate House owned over fifty per cent.

'You don't really need to know all this. All the accounts are clearly marked and Ralph looks after that side of it anyway. You just need to know how the registers are marked, up, Ralph deals with all the ins and outs of it.'

'What do I say if someone comes in and asks about finding somewhere to live, or asks after one of the places on the cards?'

'Cards, cards, here.' Maureen had opened the bottom drawer of the grey filing cabinet and brought out a small card index box. She brought it over to Rats. 'The cards are just to give an idea of the sorts of places we have. They're changed in rotation.'
She handed the box to Rats who saw that it had a range of houses, flats and bedsits in it, arranged month by month.

'They're not real then?'

'No, but we do have places like that from time to time. It's not exactly misleading.'
Maureen was quite oblivious to Rats' discomfort.

'Anyway, come in and say, "I'm looking for a flat". Go on, say it.'
Rats repeated the request.

'Well madam, if you'll just fill in this form for me, so we can see exactly what you would like and what we have to suit you, I'm sure we'll be able to help.'
She handed Rats a duplicated sheet which she glanced at. It asked far more about the person than the kind of place they wanted. Maureen paused while Rats finished reading it.

'There's no fee of course, that's illegal you know. You shouldn't pay to use an agency. We do, of course, have a small administration charge if you wish to remain on our list.'

Rats looked at Maureen, trying to remember whether agencies could or couldn't charge tenants.

'And then you take the form off them, look it over and make an appointment for them to come back. You pass that on to Ralph, he deals with actually letting places to people. You don't really have a lot to do with them, just be pleasant and helpful.'

'About how many people a day do you see?'

'It varies. Sometimes nobody, sometimes five or six. Most of your work is with people we already have on our books.'

'What happens if someone is offered a place?'

'Well, you might have to show them round, or Ralph would, depending on how busy he was. If you are going to show them round, Ralph'll tell you what to say. It varies from place to place. If they're interested you have quite a lot to do. You write off for references from their jobs, and you draw up the agreement – we have a standard agreement but we type it out each time, check the inventory, write and offer them the tenancy, get all these signed, take the money, cash or bank draft, not a cheque, and then hand over the keys.'

'Do you only take people with jobs?'

Maureen was shuffling papers, pulling out examples of tenancy agreements, showing her how a file was put together for a new tenant.

'It depends.'

Rats was looking through the file. She didn't bother to ask what it depended on. A new tenancy could cost as much as £400. Rent in advance, rent in lieu of a deposit and administration charges. Rats thought that key money had been outlawed. It looked like they'd just started to call it something else.

'We don't make people leave if they lose their jobs, as long as they can still pay the rent. It's happening a lot you know, people out of work. My brother was made redundant two years ago and he's still without. Not for want of trying either. Barry's a good worker, and he's got a house and two kiddies. He reckons if you look hard enough the work's there for the finding,' she inclined her head, dismissively towards the back room, 'him, not Barry, but I'm not so sure. They can't all be workshy layabouts, can they? And the number of shops and factories that are closing. You don't know sometimes who your neighbours are along her from one week to the next. Places opening up and closing down every other day, it seems.'

Ralph came into their part of the room and looked over Maureen's shoulders as his hands rested on them.

'Showing you the ropes is she? I hope you're managing to take it all in. Birdbrain here probably doesn't know half of what she's supposed to be doing anyway. I'll have a word with you after lunch, we close up from twelve-thirty to one-thirty.'

Rats flinched at the casual insult to Maureen but said nothing. They were both smiling. His little joke, Maureen would probably say. Rats wondered if Ralph was going to run down her work in the same way and whether she could contain her temper if he did. Ralph said he'd get her a key cut while he was out and they left the building together. Rats walked on ahead, Maureen waited for Ralph to lock up. She hadn't been invited to go with them, so she wandered off by herself to explore the cafes and snack bars close by.

She settled for Macdonald's, cheeseburger with fries and a regular coke. As she ate, she reflected on the morning. The work seemed straightforward enough. Although she felt uneasy about the nature of the work, she hadn't the luxury of fretting about it. A job was a job. Finishing her food, she set off back to work, walking slowly, taking her time to stop and look into shop windows. The prospect of a wage at the end of the week worked its illusory magic. As a wage earner she was included in the round of spending and getting. But even as she stood assessing the range of goods before her, she realised how little difference work made in terms of hard cash.

Back at the office Ralph took her into the back room. His instructions were a catalogue of what she didn't do; a filing cabinet that she need not, as he put it, mess with; the larger property owners with whom he would deal direct. This finished with, he kept her a further hour interspersing questions about her family, the past, previous jobs, her current life and opinions with a self-inflated account of the importance of their firm, and its place in larger things, significant connections and prospects. When Rats went back into the front office, Maureen was typing out records for tenants' rent. All rents were due on the fifteenth of the month, and by now they had had the bulk of them in and banked.

Rats drew up a chair beside her, to watch, then, having grasped the process gradually, worked in alongside Maureen. It kept them busy until closing time.

Ralph came through from his office, his jacket on. It looked like time to go. Maureen switched off the typewriter, Rats put down her work and self-consciously stood up to put on her coat. Nobody checked her so she said goodbye to Maureen and left. Once home, the tiredness she had been keeping on top of all afternoon hit her and she found herself, after a tea of beans on toast and two pots of tea, ready for bed just after nine o'clock.

For the rest of the week her life followed a similar pattern. She took the bus into work, worked with Maureen, chatted inconsequentially to Ralph. Gradually she got to know their likes and dislikes, opinions and prejudices. She told them little about herself. At times she felt she had, indeed, little to say. Sometimes though, she was conscious of holding back, evading certain issues, implying rather than stating attitudes, neither denying nor confirming what they believed about her. Ralph probably had her summed up as a quiet woman, waiting for the right man to happen along. A little odd, perhaps, but nothing wrong with her, pleasant enough, probably good with children. Later, when he felt sufficiently familiar with her he might even go so far as to suggest she wear some make-up or an occasional frock. After all, he knew what a man liked. Maureen, on the other hand, had not asked about boyfriends. Her silence on the matter was firm and not unfriendly.

Rats bought a paper every lunch hour. Tuesday and Friday she bought the *Hackney Gazette*, other days she bought a *Standard*. She bought them partly to have something to look at as she sat in the various cafes she frequented at lunch times, but also because she continued to believe that some day, somewhere, she was going to read about a dead body, in a car, in north-east London. She never did.

4

It was a shock when some weeks later, sitting on the bus in a queue of morning traffic, she saw the Rolls. At first, looking out of the window, she had just taken quiet satisfaction in the visible annoyance and irritation of the driver. He revved the engine, tapped his fingers on the wheel, rocked forward as if sheer aggression could force his car through the immovable streams of traffic. Suddenly the traffic cleared. As the car surged forward she recognised it. The same dark green Rolls Royce. The knowledge sent a rush of adrenalin round her body, hitting an empty stomach. She felt sick, a child anxiously waiting for the home stop. Sitting, breathing slowly, she tried to remember the man. Perhaps it was him, not dead as she thought but injured, recovered, driving about in his car. The incident unsettled her, but not for long. Maureen gossiped with her over tea.

'You're a good worker, you are. I was saying to Ralph this weekend, you're good, I'm going to stop after this week. I'll pop in every once in a while but you've got the hang of it.'

Rats smiled at her. 'You should stop really, you don't want to take any chances.'

Ralph joined them for the tea break. They discussed the areas of work Maureen had trained her in, the ones she had still no experience of. Rats said she felt she could manage the work, the only thing she was concerned about was dealing with people coming into the office.

'What's the problems there?' Ralph asked.

'Well, partly that no one ever comes in, I don't know what I'd say if they did. I mean I've got used to the ones wandering in trying to sell *War Cry* and *Newsline* and God knows what else, and the ones who want to chat and the religious ones and the loopy ones and the lonely ones. But no one's been in here after a place to live since I started to work here.'

Ralph looked momentarily uncomfortable, then he beamed at her. 'My problem that, not yours, I'm still paying your wages, aren't I?'

It was Maureen who answered her directly. 'It's not a lot of our work, the people. These flats run themselves in a way. We don't get many new properties, at least not vacant ones, and then there's the referrals.'

For the rest of the week Rats worked at routine jobs that kept the office running smoothly. She took a pride in keeping things efficient, knowing what needed to be done and then doing it. She liked to see a pile of typed letters awaiting Ralph's signature; an empty 'to be filed' tray; a balanced petty cash book. It was rare, of course, that each day ran so smoothly. There were little interruptions from the passers-by who saw a shop front office as an invitation to pass the time of day, letters Ralph remembered halfway through the morning that needed to be in the lunchtime post, all the bustle and chaos and predictability of any job. But in the main, Rats and Maureen kept things well regulated, their work was largely invisible to Ralph, he would notice it only when it ceased to be done.

As Friday was to be Maureen's last, the three of them went to a nearby pub, to toast the baby's health. Rats was surprised at the rate Maureen drank gin and lime, but Maureen assured her nothing harmed a baby after the first three months. Rats was beginning to feel a bit light-headed. Her two halves of bitter and a whiskey and dry had gone straight to her head. She felt, though, she should get a round of drinks before she went. She had just finished asking what they wanted when a voice from behind her said: 'This one's on me, what'll it be? Something special, eh?'

The accent was curious, not English, not quite American but closer to that than anything else. Ralph, looking up, clearly recognised the man.

'Cruze, what are you doing here? Sit down, let me get you a drink.' Rats turned to see a well-dressed, middle-aged man. Ralph and he acted out a little ritual of hands on shoulders, restraining the other from producing his wallet, and the inviting into seats. Rats decided she'd let them settle who was paying for this round. They walked over to the bar together.

'Who's that?' she asked Maureen.

'That's Cruze. He owns our firm, sort of lets it to us. He's a lovely man, sophisticated. Very nice man he is.'

Cruze returned with doubles all round and a large plate of beef sandwiches. Maureen introduced her. As she took his hand Rats felt a fleeting recognition. It was a ridiculous idea, she didn't come across men like this, if anything the recognition would be for a certain kind of advertising style; Dior Aftershave, Rover cars and fine malt whiskeys. That's where she had seen him before. He had their slick air of money, that same superficiality.

Cruze had come by specially to wish Maureen well. He had presents for her and the baby, a generous bagful, gift-wrapped by Harrods. The talk was all of the baby, what sex they would prefer, what they were going to call it, what the probability was of it having red hair. Cruze seemed genuinely interested in Maureen, Ralph and the baby. Rats felt unkind in her dismissal of him as slick and shallow. She found herself wondering if he was married, had children of his own. Rats took a back seat in the conversation, excluded as she was by her unfamiliarity.

19

At half-past eight Cruze left them, he had promised to meet people in town. He offered lifts, but they were all going in different directions. Ralph and Maureen persuaded Rats to join them in one for the road, Rats persuaded them to let her call them a taxi in that case. The bargain struck, Rats finally bought her round of drinks. When she returned with them, Ralph and Maureen were talking privately. With the clumsiness of people the worse for wear for drink, they broke off mid-sentence, embarrassed. Rats apologised, for what she wasn't quite sure. Maureen looked as if she might have told her but Ralph intervened: 'A toast to the baby,' he raised his glass.

'And to the mother.'

'And the father – whoever he was,' added Maureen as they downed their drinks in one.

Rats decided against sharing their taxi. She was relaxed and in good spirits, she thought she would go on down to the club. It was Friday night after all.

Rats didn't often go to the club on her own. She felt self-conscious, nervous of asking anyone to dance, terrified of being asked. She hadn't the ease of joining casually in conversation with strangers, distinguishing friendly overtures from those more overtly sexual. And she didn't deal very well with either of them. It amazed her, sometimes, how she had ever found herself a girlfriend. But then, she hadn't found her in a small and sleazy club hidden away beneath the city's streets. Tonight though, she just felt like the company, the music and more to drink.

When she got to 'The Out-Dyke' the happy hour was long gone. But she still ordered a cocktail anyway. They served the cheapest, maybe the worst, cocktails in London. Worst, that is, if you drank your cocktails for the trimmings because there were none. The drinks came in ordinary glasses, a rough assortment of the required liquors mixed in over ice and served with a straw and a paper parasol. Tonight Rats' parasol was turquoise. As she opened it out, sipping her drink and glancing around she wondered whether the parasols were made by hand or machine. She wondered what it would be like to make them day in, day out. Whether you would have a favourite colour. Whether you wondered about the people whose drinks they adorned.

Rats was conscious of being watched, a woman at one of the tables kept looking over, trying to make eye contact. As she succeeded in doing so, Rats smiled. It was the woman from the International

Supermarket where she often bought her groceries on the way home. Rats picked up her drink and walked over.

'Hello, you do come in our shop, don't you?' said the woman clearing a coat from a chair for Rats.

Rats nodded.

'I thought so, have a seat. My friends are dancing. Here on your own?'

'Yes, just thought I'd look in.'

She was about twenty-five. She was unremarkable at work, just another overalled woman with her name plate – Mrs Morris, Rats remembered – who tapped your purchases into the computerised cash register, wrapped the perishables in clear plastic bags and handed you your change. Hour after hour, day after day.

'I thought I'd say hello. We should stick together, shouldn't we. I thought you might be, but I'd never say it to a customer. Get me the sack probably. Do you live near Mare Street?'

'No, I work there. I live in Stoke Newington.'

'Nice there, I've got friends who live on the George Downing and the Northwold. Good estates they are, better than where I am.'

'Where's that?'

'Nightingale Estate.'

There wasn't a lot to be said about living on Nightingale. Massed concrete, chrome and glass that rose high and wide above a very small area of land. It had a reputation for vandalism, isolation and damp.

'That must be rough.'

'You get used to it. I've lived there for fifteen years, since I was a kid. We moved in when they pulled the old houses down. You wouldn't have known this place then, it was so different. Can you imagine Hackney without tower blocks? I can't remember what it was like really.'

Rats offered to buy her a drink, which she accepted. When she returned, Rats introduced herself.

'I only know you as Mrs Morris.'

'Oh that, that's not my name. It's the name of the woman who had the job before me. I inherited her job, locker, overalls and name tags. I'll be getting my own soon – Liz Murray. Where is it you work then?'

'The property managers' place.'

Liz raised her eyebrows, 'That place!'

'What's up with it?'

'Nothing, I don't know anything about it really.'

21

'You know enough to pull a face.'

'Well, just gossip. People are always out for other people. It's probably not true.'

'So what've you heard?'

'That they're not all they look. You know, a front for something. Nobody ever goes in there, do they?'

'No but we collect rents.'

'I didn't say you didn't. But do you know what they're for?'

'No. I've only been there a couple of weeks, and it's temporary, while the woman's off having a baby.'

'Well, in that case don't take any notice. Like I say, people make up stories, especially men. It was my brother told me about them. He fancies himself as a bit of a villain. East End's full of them. Petty thieves who've got even bigger than usual dreams about what they're doing and who they know and where it's going to get them. Got a lot to answer for, whoever first spread the word that the East End villain's any smarter or tougher than anywhere else's. They're all as thick and vicious as the next one.'

'But how was your brother involved with them then?'

'He wasn't. It was just a little fiddle, him and a mate were thinking of getting in on, opening a hotel but taking the bed and breakfast trade. They were warned off from the place you work for. I don't know why I remembered it. Probably just because you work there. Douggie's been warned off more fiddles than you or I've had hot dinners. He probably made the whole thing up, just picked them because of that bloody great neon sign. Do you want another drink?'

It was nearly closing time. Rats, conscious of the effects of the evening's drinking, felt she should leave but agreed to another. While Liz was at the bar her friends came back to the table. They introduced themselves briefly and surreptitiously eyed her up. The bar was crowded now and the music louder. The ceiling was low, being a cellar bar, and the music seemed to bounce around it. The atmosphere had lost its edginess, everyone was well into enjoying themselves or appearing to. When Liz returned with their drinks the conversation became more general, more flirtatious. Rats was offered a lift home with them, invited back to someone's house where there was rumoured to be a party. She declined. Agreeing to go to the party felt like more than she was ready for, she didn't want to let Liz down.

The 73 she caught was going to Tottenham Garage. That meant it stopped on Stamford Hill, not the Common. It was surprisingly busy as she waited to cross at the zebra, plenty of cars in either direction, groups of people milling about on their way home from pubs or going on to clubs and parties. As she crossed, Rats thought she caught a glimpse of the car, the Rolls. By the time she'd reached the pavement and turned around she could only make out the familiar shape, the tail lights disappearing. It could have been the car, it could have been some other Rolls Royce. They were commoner than she could ever have guessed, passing through Hackney on their way home to the leafy suburbs of Hertfordshire. Rats walked on up Caitlin Road, a slight tingle across her skin. Nothing she couldn't cope with.

5

Rats settled into a routine that was comfortable and untaxing. She went to work every day and spent her weekends at home, reading and pottering around her flat. Work was different without Maureen, less companionable. Ralph missed her; at times he looked like a lost sheep, plaintive and confused. Rats' fears about his lechery remained unfounded. She, too, missed Maureen's energy and warmth. Yet it wasn't all isolation. She occasionally met Liz from work and they went out together to drink and dance. They enjoyed each other's company but it went no further.

As the evenings started to lighten and the air to lift, Rats felt a peace descend. She was happy in her life, a fragile sort of contentment, but important to her. It was St Patrick's Day and she was tempted by a women's ceilidh but decided against it. She played her Fureys' record several times by way of marking the celebration.

Throughout the evening she avoided silence. The record player for the housework, the radio, then the TV, then the record player again. She was used to noise, had grown up in a boisterous household, found silences unsettling. As she lay on her bed, reading a library book, her mind drifted idly around her main preoccupation – her job and the death.

The job lay as agreeably on her mind as unemployment had discomforted it. The death was something else. She still scanned the newspapers, but with no longer any real hope of seeing the news story she looked for. And, as always, she questioned whether she'd really seen what she had. But, she reassured herself, she couldn't have imagined that scene. It was too bizarre and improbable to be fictitious. She thought about the car. She had seen it about Hackney enough to have recognised it that evening, and then seen it another two or three times since. Rats wanted to know who drove that car, how long they'd owned it. She wondered whether the blood stains had come out of the leather upholstery.

She lay there, the sky dark outside and her harsh bulb lighting the room around her. She thought about bringing the cat in, making a cup of tea and going to bed. She puzzled over tracking down the car's owner. If I could drive, she thought, I could drive into it. Then exchange insurance policy numbers, names and addresses. To the accompaniment of such idle speculation, Rats went through the rituals of preparing for bed – the cat called in, teeth brushed, lights out.

The next day felt warm, like spring for the first time. Rats decided to take a walk through the cemetery to the park. She followed the broad, gravelled path as far as the first triangle of graves. Daughters killed in car accidents, fathers who fell asleep, grandmothers at peace, all marked by elaborate stone monuments. An open book, two doors ajar, leading not to the gates of heaven but to unkempt cluttered graves, obelisks and memorials. Bouquets of flowers set apart those who cared from those content to let their duty rest at burial. The cemetery was cut through with paths, overgrown with brambles, grasses and young trees. The outer rims had a well-kept path, wide enough for the funeral hearse to creep its way round to the appointed plot. The inner paths led deeper in, creating the illusion that the cemetery was larger than it was. Rats set off down a path she hoped would bring her to the gate on Church Street.

As she paused by a headstone something moved, just out of vision. Turning she saw a pregnant brown rat scuttle from one grave to another. It sat in the sun, rested on its haunches and washed its face. Rats watched it out of sight. It paused, then pushed on into the long grass growing by the side of a rubbish dump, scraps of paper, plastic and organic matter heaped together.

It made her shudder, yet there was nothing repellent about it. It looked healthy, clean and content. Domesticated, they were

24

supposed to make intelligent, loyal pets. She thought of her nickname, Rats, and compared herself to that creature, stealthy and at ease in the stench and decay of urban living, growing sleek and reproducing. Perhaps it was the sunlight that had affected her. The province of rats, was, after all, the sewers and the slums.

She got the name through her moodiness and her hair. 'Ratface' Helen had called her, trying to coax her out of a sulky, sullen mood, 'Little Ratface' and despite her protests it had become Rats and stuck, as much a part of her now as the straggly hair that hung, wet or dry, like rats' tails down her back. Her family and schoolfriends, her workmates, never knew her as anything other than Gerry. Good old dependable Gerry. The sort you were grateful to have for the last minute babysitting or to sit with a sick relation. The one you could never quite appreciate as you ought and would, if anything, mock for their willingness to put themselves out for others. Just as she was Gerry to them, to her lesbian friends she was nothing but Rats – strong and silent, who held her drink and kept her head: coming or going as she pleased, on her own or with Helen, as tall as she was short, as slim as she was broad, as frivolous and friendly and down-to-earth as she was not. A cold fish? Maybe. Like many a person hunched in the prison of denim and leather she was more sensitive than she'd ever dare admit, especially to herself.

Leaving the cemetery, Rats bought a *Sunday Mirror* on Church Street. Reaching the park she walked around the animal enclosures, poking two fingers through to feel the velvet muzzles of the roe deer and the rabbits. They sniffed and breathed into her hand, but finding it empty of food moved on. There was a cluster of people, mostly toddlers with parents, clutching carrots or cabbage leaves, trailing packets of bread crusts. Rats stopped and looked in on the guinea pigs and peacocks, the hens scratching in their already bare enclosures.

At the cafe she bought a cup of tea and a hot dog which she took outside to eat, sitting in the shelter of the terrace, looking out over the stream, the crocuses just coming through along its edges. She spread the newspaper, glancing at the usual sex and scandal. Her attention was caught by a demonstration in Tower Hamlets the day before. It had been called by the Bengali community to protest against the Council's reluctance to rehouse families suffering racial harassment. The demonstration had sparked off a march by the British Movement under the slogan 'Fair Play for Whites'. There was a picture of three separate groups of people. In the foreground, five youths with short cropped hair and t-shirts, one with a Union Jack motif, another with a Bulldog. Behind them, a line of police wearing their expressionless faces and behind them, almost out of the picture, a line of Bengali faces and banners that blurred, with the newsprint, into an indistinct mass.

Someone had been killed, there was to be an inquest. The family's mourning, dragged through the maze of officialdom, made a thing apart from them, to be duly witnessed, adjudged, sealed and stamped.

As she sat flicking through the paper, she felt uncomfortable, a spectator on the miseries and misfortunes of the world. There was no news to speak of in the paper, just a catalogue of sexual infidelities, falls from grace, and deaths. She remembered what it had been like when her elder brother's conviction for burglary had been in the local paper. How much more devastating than that to have the photographs and the indiscretions; interpretations put upon the squalid, sometimes bumbling ways of living and loving. And, looking at the face of a dead child, Rats wondered what it must be like to read a paragraph summing up your child, or lover, their life, their death.

She read a short item about the death, apparently in a suicide pact, of two lovers. They had both died as a result of gunshot wounds in Epping Forest six or seven weeks ago. The verdict was accidental death. She folded the paper over and left it on the table as she rose to continue her stroll. As she walked she realised that even if she did one day recognise a face staring out from the newspaper, it would tell her nothing.

That evening, and for part of the following week, the death and the car receded for her. Then she started to notice the car again, in traffic, gliding through the streets, sometimes parked at a garage, outside buildings. One evening, coming back from the library she saw it at the bottom of her road, in the same place as on that night. She stopped to steady her breathing, her legs shaky. She watched people pass by the car, not giving it a second glance, until she felt able to walk past it, looking inside to check it was empty.

6

Housing benefit was introduced in the spring. Rats was surprised it affected them. The lettings were geared to those in work. But while they could regulate tenants coming in, they could not evict people when they lost their jobs – until they fell behind with their rents, that is. People were losing jobs at an alarming rate. It could happen to anybody and they all had to live somewhere. The unemployed existed as shadows behind workers, ghosts whispering in their ears, breathing over their shoulders. Rats tried to fit faces and bodies to these figures: to fill in their families and friends, ambitions, emotions, life. She could not do it. The sheer weight of pain, the deadening waste of hope, energy and enthusiasm drew a shroud across the faces, closed the door on their lives. The first she knew of housing benefit was Ralph's set face, his smile gone. As a rule he was genial, easy-going.

'What've I done then? Get it out and I'll see what I can do,' Rats put down her biro, looking him square in the face as she spoke.

'It's not you, Gerry. It's this bloody government. Why someone can't tell that woman where to get off I don't know. Call themselves men, there isn't a man worthy of the name in that party.'

It was rare that Ralph expounded his views on politics. Rats sat waiting for the diatribe against VAT, income tax, the conduct of the Falklands War, Ireland, Law and Order. She didn't, as Ralph did, hate Thatcher for being a woman. But she enjoyed urging Ralph on, trying to get him to see that his distaste for the leader ought to extend to the party itself. As she gathered her thoughts in preparation Ralph continued: 'It's a right mess. It'll take months to sort out and we'll be the ones losing money.'

'What's up, Ralph?'

'Social security. I don't know why they don't just abolish it. That'd solve some of the unemployment, get those cushy buggers off their arses, put a stop to all these girls having kids just to jump the waiting list for council flats. But no, they're too bloody scared of who voted them in and can vote them out.'

'Ralph . . . '

'Social security. Right, you're on social security and they pay you your rent. Then you pay your landlord. Straightforward enough, same as wages. If you don't pay up out of your money – courtesy of the social security, *my money* – I'll have you out, eventually and get in someone who can and does pay.'

The various stages of this argument were emphasised by much hand waving and beating upon the desk with the pile of papers Ralph had brought in.

'So what's changed?'

'I'm making some coffee. I'll explain it then.' Ralph started to make coffee. He was one of those men who believed that if he did a thing slowly, or clumsily, or badly enough, especially a domestic task, someone, usually a woman, would sweep him briskly aside to complete the job herself. He slopped water out of the kettle, looked puzzled by the absence of clean mugs, forgot to switch the kettle on, spilt coffee on the floor. Rats was one of those women who could wait indefinitely for a cup of coffee produced under such circumstances.

When it finally appeared, Ralph sat down. Rats looked at him expectantly.

'It's some cock-eyed scheme to simplify rent, they say. All rent for people on social security is now going to be paid through the local authority.'

'What's the problem with that?'

'Well, one problem is that lot down at the Town Hall. How long do you think it's going to take them to sort out something like this? Six months? A year? They're all too busy wasting my money on street festivals and making Hackney a Nuclear Free Zone. I hope they've told Russia that, that we're nuclear free, so they'll know to leave us alone when they get trigger happy with their missiles. Hackney Goes Local? Hackney goes Loco.'

Rats sighed, her only contribution to the discussion. She had been to one of the street festivals and quite enjoyed herself. 'I don't see why you're worrying. It sounds as if you're guaranteed your rent.'

'It's not that simple. Some of the tenancies, it comes direct to us, others it goes to them. Either way, changing like this is unnecessary.'

Rats supposed she should ask whether it meant her doing anything different. Before she could, he started speaking again. Not the irate tone of the last twenty minutes. He sounded worried. Rats paid attention.

'They have limits now as well. They only pay so much of the rent and they decide how much. We could lose money hand over fist.'

Rats wasn't sympathetic. She thought the rents too high. 'Is this going to mean new work for me?'

'I don't know yet. What I could do with is a list of all tenants who aren't working, would we know that?'

'Only if they've let us know. They do, usually, to explain delays paying the rent.'

'You could check on them for me. Do that. Start tomorrow, finish what you're working on now. Tomorrow I want you to go through and check everyone's work references, it should be easy enough. You could just ask to speak to them. You'll think of some excuse.'
Ralph sounded excited. It would reassure him to think they were doing something. He would enjoy having his list of those in and out of work. His hit list, Rats thought, feeling uncomfortable. 'Is it necessary?' she found herself saying. 'What would be the point of it?'
Ralph bristled.

'It's not for you to say. I know why I want the list, just you concentrate on getting it for me. A week should be ample time. Leave the thinking to me.'
He had gathered up the papers and returned to his office, composure ruffled. Rats picked up one of the leaflets that he'd left behind. She glanced at it. The usual long-winded legalistic jargon. She didn't understand it. Putting the leaflet to one side, she continued with her interrupted work. She was providing trial balances for the end of year accounts. As her eyes strained across the figures, she fumed at Ralph. She had more work to do on the balance than he recognised and she did not relish checking on the tenants. But she had, throughout her life, learnt the merit of holding her peace.

It was lunchtime before Rats completed the trial balances.

'You can start on that list now. Tell people we're making an insurance return, they can't quibble with that. You can manage that, can you?' His sarcasm showed he hadn't forgotten their skirmish. Rats felt her colour rise. She approached Ralph directly, appealing to his compassion. It was not a wise move. 'Ralph I don't want to do this. It feels mean and dishonest. We've no right to check up on people like this. It's hard enough losing a job without being hounded by your landlord. Can't we just leave it?'

'Gerry, I told you yesterday, I'm telling you now and if needs be I'll tell you tomorrow. And tomorrow if you still need telling, I'll find someone else. You know what I'm going to say. I want that information and I want you to get it for me. That is your job, doing what I tell you. You'd do well to worry about your own work, not other people's. Is that clear?'

The atmosphere was tense.

'Perfectly clear, Ralph.'

She said it as calmly as she could and left the room.

Back at her desk she took the index of tenants and started to copy a list of names. She filled eight sheets of paper, 248 names to check. The business was busier than she imagined. Asked to estimate their clients, she would have put the figure at about half that. She worked out the average yearly income, £350,000. The figure niggled her. Jealous, she told herself, ruling the page into columns, one to write the place of work, one to tick if working. As she ruled the last page up she realised why the figure irked her. It didn't add up. She had just balanced the year's books, she remembered the total payments, £220,200. All those 2s, she kept getting her noughts and points in the wrong place.

Well, she thought, sitting back wondering how best to assemble the details she needed, the books must be right, they'd been kept properly. She put the thought out of her mind. She decided to work through the files, transferring the information. It delayed the moment when she was going to have to pick up that phone and start prying into other people's lives. It occurred to her to write 'yes' by all the names but it wouldn't fool Ralph, alert to her resistance. She wouldn't put it past him to check her findings at random. The work had to be done properly.

It took longer than anticipated to complete the list. By Friday afternoon she was ready to start phoning. Ralph had wanted it completed by Monday. Things had been strained between them all week, they made even less effort than usual, their conversation was minimal. On Friday they hadn't had a single cup of coffee, each wanting to avoid a repeat of the previous day's frosty breaks. There were staccato questions and answers about Maureen and the pregnancy. Rats ostentatiously kept busy; Ralph, uncomfortable in the role of domineering boss, was nevertheless able to play it with ease. It had the familiarity of an old leather glove, a smooth fit once the initial tugging had secured it.

Just after three o'clock Rats made coffee, asking Ralph if he wanted one. She took the mug through to him and putting the coffee down she spoke, 'Ralph, it's not that I'm dragging my heels, but you'll be

30

pushed to have that list by this time next week. It's a big job.'

'That's okay. I can see you're doing it despite what you think. I don't know what happened this week, we seemed to be getting on fine. I hope it's not the start of, well, you know.' He paused. 'I'd be sorry to have to let you go.'

Rats figured it was the closest she was going to get to an apology.

'I'm not planning on going anywhere,' she said 'I reckon the weekend's all we need.'

Ralph smiled and raised his coffee mug in mock salute, touching it to her, 'Cheers.'

'The weekend.'

'The weekend.'

They each took a mouthful. 'And Monday morning,' grinned Rats.

'There'll be no one in to phone now,' said Ralph, 'why don't you just finish off and go when you're ready?'

'Thanks, I will, see you then.'

Rats was pleased she had the courage to make amends. The issue was not resolved, she felt no better about what she was being asked to do. But the fact of the matter was she would have to go on working there, like it or not, and it was easier if there was some meeting ground, however slight between herself and Ralph.

She appreciated leaving early. She could go down to York Hall and take a Turkish bath. The bath's last ticket was sold at five-thirty which meant if you were working you could never get there. She felt her body relax, just anticipating the steamy, stupefying heat, the magnificent variety of the other women. The quiet confidences of smiles, the brief conversations. Imagining the pleasure to come she felt a small stirring in her stomach, a glimmer of a memory. The steam baths in Hull and her rare trips there with Helen. Their careful embraces in the resting cubicles, the sense of regret she had for other women, that they could not share her pleasure in her lover's body, feeling herself shimmer and open in her presence, their guarded intimacy in such naked, public places. She surprised herself, letting the memory ride and flood her body with sensations damped off, kept down. Such is the way of desire.

31

7

On Monday, Rats began phoning through the list. By eleven-thirty she wondered how long she'd last. The excuse she was using sounded pathetic. Once someone said that she could check the insurance from the rent receipts and what did she really want. Rats panicked, apologised profusely and hung up. She checked over the morning's work. Out of fifteen calls, ten people were in work, two definitely weren't and three were unclear. She could calculate a probability from that, but she was still wary of Ralph checking on her. At this rate, it was going to take more than a week to get through the list. She picked up the receiver and dialled the next in line. She was going to do five more then switch to another task before going out to lunch.

As the week progressed, Rats found her job harder to do. The routine work had to be hurried, done perfunctorily. The pressure was on to complete the check. More often than not there was a complicated route to establish who she wanted to talk with, where they were, when they'd left and where they'd gone. Usually this was done with a persistent kindness by the people Rats called, testifying to the boredom and routine nature of their working lives. Rats pushed beyond her own limits, determined to finish the job.

By Thursday she was almost there. The number of people presumed or actually out of work surprised Rats. It was much higher than she would have guessed, almost half. On Friday her familiar pleasure at the prospect of the weekend was marred. Sad and angry at the complete list, Rats found little satisfaction in having finished the job. It was a betrayal. The files held less than a dozen letters concerning delayed rents. She was helping to put the finger on people already pushed down, singled out. People always put rent first, especially in London where somewhere, anywhere to live was at a premium. Ralph always got his money, and good money for overpriced, badly maintained property. But he could never trust that. Living on people's fears, he could never trust the power of the fear he exercised over them. She felt a bad taste in her mouth, a sense of apprehension about what she was letting them in for. She put the finishing touches to the list and took it into Ralph.

Giving it a cursory glance, he put it to one side. 'I'll be seeing to that next week.'

She stood framed in the doorway.

'It looks very thorough, you can do a good job when you set your mind to it.' He gave her an appraising look, discomforting.

'You could do better for yourself than this job. Smarten up a bit, try for the City or West End. Ever work up West?'

This wasn't the discussion Rats expected or wanted.

'What will you be doing with the list?'

'Monday, Gerry. Give it a rest now. Don't let it spoil your weekend, will you. How about a coffee? You'll be wanting something to do for the rest of the afternoon.'

He smiled, a lecherous sort of smile, his form of communication. As Rats backed out of his office into her own she was furious. For a brief moment he had not distinguished her from Maureen. The demands for coffee, cigarettes, the smoothing out of his life, were a tape running on automatic, programmed with appropriate endearing gestures. She felt she'd lost not just that particular skirmish, but the tolerable working relationship she had with Ralph. He was a man, she was a woman, he was in charge, she was to be told, bullied, cajoled, worked. The circle of Maureen's protection had finally worn out. She was on her own now.

Over coffee, Rats broached a subject which bothered her.

'It was interesting doing this list. Gave me a good grasp of the business. But it was odd, doing it just after the books. They, you know, didn't seem to match up.'

Ralph stiffened, or perhaps she imagined it, so easy was it now to see him as malicious, a parasite. An unpleasant man doing an unpleasant job.

'How d'ye work that out?'

'I did the balance. I remember that figure because it was such a performance finding it. I also know what our average rents are. The numbers of people and the rents don't add up.'

'I think you must have exaggerated the number of phone calls you had to make. It's hardly likely that we've been forgetting to collect rents.'

'Maybe. It doesn't feel right though.'

Ralph patted the ledger book in front of him. 'I'll sort it out then, I'll find out if there's anything wrong. You must be going off the deep end a bit. You just didn't like that job, did you? Why don't you come and have a drink after work? Celebrate finishing it?'

Rats was on the point of refusing; he saw the hesitation, 'Maureen was saying last night she'd like to see you. She's picking me up. It gets lonely for her at home.'

'Love to,' said Rats, 'it'll be nice to see her again.'

Rats was pleased to be seeing Maureen. It was only because of her that she had ended up working here. There was something vibrant about her. How women like that ended up with men like Ralph was beyond Rats. She went back to her desk, contemplating such oddities, as she got on with a few end-of-week jobs.

The drink was pleasant, they stayed for about an hour and a half. Maureen was proud of her pregnancy and looked well with it. Her hair and skin glowed, her belly thrust out in front of her. Rats felt jaded and dull by comparison.

Rats was spending a quiet weekend. She usually did. Partly it was the need to rest after the week, partly it was a different phase of grieving for Helen. She had been through the first, almost exhilarating phases of drinking too much, too often. Finally, Rats had to face her loss. She went back a long way with Helen, and Helen would always be different for her, because she was her first lover. The wildness when she first came to London was almost a way of punishing herself. They had both talked about London; the excitement, the freedom. Everything had come to hang on the move and when it came, Rats had come alone, bitter and betrayed. Helen had been unable to break away from the city she had grown up in; London, she finally admitted, scared her. Now Rats retreated from the city. She had a few friends, but the clubs and bars bored her. The surface interactions no longer satisfied. She felt like a beginner trying to go deeper. Over the seven years she and Helen were together, they had relied on each other for companionship, love, friendship, sex. Those friends that had known about them found it hard to accept and as they married and children arrived, connections were strained past breaking point. Rats and Helen were driven further into dependence on each other. Alone now, she couldn't risk that again. Emptiness and despair lay at the edges of her mind. From time to time she recognised her state as mourning, an ache for the past.

As the weeks passed she settled into a more comfortable existence, no longer gripped by the panic she had lived with immediately after discovering the body. She no longer read the papers so avidly, no longer searched for the car. It was almost forgotten, settling into the sediment of memory. Rats was glad to be back in her usual routine. Opening mail, dealing with letters, checking on some repairs that had been put in hand. Ralph was busy in the back office. At lunchtime he shut up office but didn't go out; instead he asked her to bring him back a sandwich. Setting off for her own amble around the shops in search of a cafe, she wondered what he was working on. It was unusual for Ralph to work through without a break.

When Rats got back to the office with Ralph's ham and salad sandwich, she found him waiting for her. He had drafted a letter which he wanted her to send to each unemployed person on the list. It was a brief letter, drawing attention to the original agreement made between Lindy's and the tenant in the employment of a named organisation. It stated that failure to comply with any of the clauses revoked the agreement. It was not a letter that warranted the morning spent on its composition. It was a threatening letter, the more so because those receiving it weren't to know Lindy's knew they were unemployed and, in an ungenerous interpretation, already in breach of their agreements. Ralph waited while she read it.

Rats was surprised to hear herself say, 'Couldn't we at least wait until they start falling behind with their rent? Or why not serve a notice to quit on the whole bloody lot of them? Have you ever thought about losing your job, Ralph, what it might feel like? It's not a crime or a moral depravity. It's not their fault.'

'Those letters are to be sent. It's for you to type them. If you don't want to do it then I'll easily find someone who does. We've had this argument already, Gerry, I'm getting bored with it. If you want to be a social worker then try the Town Hall, they're crying out for people like you. There's plenty of call for good works round here if you're stupid enough to think you can help those who won't help themselves.'

'I can't see why you need to do it. It's not as if you're going to evict any of them. You'd look ridiculous if you took anyone to court with this sort of complaint. I'll type the bloody letters. I just want you to know I'm doing it against my will.'

'I don't have to listen to your objections, Gerry, and why I'm doing it is no business of yours. I don't consult with you. I have no need, let alone inclination to do so. And I'm getting fed up with this constant arguing. It was never like this before.'

'It wouldn't have been, would it?'

Rats felt ashamed of herself as soon as she spoke. She had a word in her head – 'wife' – that bore no relation to the spirited independence this man's wife actually had.

They stood looking at each other, fury between them. It was a moment when Rats should have walked out, but the faceless ranks of the unemployed were, in a sense, pressing their noses up against the plate-glass window. Her solidarity went so far and no further. She picked up the piece of paper.

'I'll need extra paper to do this job. And it'll take time. I take it you want them typed individually?'

'Yes, I do.'

He left the room. Rats, sitting behind her typewriter, decided to register with an agency, decided to leave. On her terms.

8

There was a constant bickering between Ralph and Rats that threatened but never quite became a full-scale row. Ralph alternated between nagging after the letters, which emerged with deliberate slowness from Rats' typewriter, and complaining about the neglect of the routine office tasks. Rats negotiated these demands upon her as best she could. When she got to work on Thursday morning Ralph was there before her. He was agitated, more so than he had been all week. They drank a cup of coffee with all the latent hostility of the week.

'This place is a mess,' said Ralph placing his coffee cup on the counter as a contribution to it.

'I've been busy, remember?'

'Can you clean it up? This morning.'

'While I type these letters,' Rats indicated the pile with her arm, 'and open the mail and deal with the phone and the customers?'

'Yes. We've got visitors. He's going to be here around twelve. He's an important man. It matters to me that he's satisfied and it'll matter to you. He doesn't like mess. And he'll have no compunction about asking you to toddle off. It's up to you.'

Ralph retreated back to his desk. Rats sourly began to clear around the room, starting with the grimy coffee area. She tidied and wiped and rearranged. She swept the floor.

'Do you want me to go out for flowers?' she called as she stopped back to admire her work, considering it finished. The sarcasm was unmistakable in her voice.

'Good idea. Better get a vase as well. Or a plant pot.'
Or even a potted plant, she thought, as she let herself out.

It didn't take long to decide on an Easter cactus from Marks and Spencer. She walked back, wondering about the visitor. She recognised him at once. It was the man who had come on Maureen's last day, Mr Pershing. He was as amiably suave now as he had been then.

'Getting on well? Fine, fine.'
Ralph, alerted by his voice came through, one hand extended, the other ushering him forward. Rats offered coffee, smiling. Ralph looked relieved. Perhaps he had been worried that she would start to rant. Perhaps she should have done. Seeing the two of them together, it was clear Ralph was in awe of Pershing. He had the upper hand. The letters were either at his insistence or designed to impress him, demonstrate initiative. A sign of the resolute manager.

Rats, secure now in her decision to leave, let it ride. She'd been wrong to elevate her expectations of the job. It was functional, a way of paying the rent. After all, it was only until Maureen returned. There was no great investment in it.

There was a low hum of voices, mostly Pershing's, from the back office. Rats took the time to stare across her desk and out the window. Occasionally she'd meet the gaze of someone scanning the cards, looking at houses too expensive for them, or killing time, or pretending to be waiting for someone. Sometimes she'd smile, sometimes she wouldn't. She turned her attention back to her desk, started entering the rent payments that were coming in, phoned to make Ralph an appointment to check the progress of the repairs on the house in Medina Road. Ralph came through to tell her to take her lunch break, he would lock up. Rats gathered her bag and jacket and went outside. She walked down towards the main shopping area. As she went past Fortescue Avenue she thought she saw the car. She walked down into the street to make sure. It was the same one, dark green. A Y registration. 'Why indeed,' she thought, the fear returning with the memory of the body. The street was empty, Rats walked up to the car and tried the doors furtively. They were all locked. She peered through the darkened glass, she could see nothing. She stood near the car, overwhelmed with the desire to touch it, to trace in its sleek solid lines the truth of having seen it before.

She checked herself. Anyone seeing her would think she was trying to steal it. She thought of pinning a message to the wiper. What would it say? 'Who are you?', 'I know about the body', 'You didn't get away with it'? And would she leave an address, her name? Of course she wouldn't. Rats thought about taking up a position and waiting for the driver to appear. She could hardly walk out of her job simply by standing in the street, waiting to see who came to claim this car. Especially not on a day when Pershing was making his presence felt around the office. She decided not to go down to the shops but to get a sandwich from one of the snack bars and come back and watch. She stood, self consciously, at the far end of the street, trying to look as if she wasn't simply standing around. It wasn't easy. She wished she had a newspaper or that there was a bench she could sit on. She tried leaning up against the street corner but found it uncomfortable. She tried pacing a route that always kept the car in sight, but felt that people would wonder what she was doing. She was conscious of drawing attention to herself. The car remained where it was.

At five to one she went back to the office. Cruze and Ralph were still in conference so she settled to work. After an hour or so she decided to go down to the Post Office for stamps. She checked with Ralph. He seemed preoccupied. The desk was covered in papers, lists of figures and addresses. He okayed her going, asked her to lock up as she went out. They didn't want to be disturbed. The car was still there when she passed it. She hoped the Post Office would be empty so she could take some time to stand and watch the car. She could always say there were queues. Mind you, the way Ralph was he didn't look like he'd notice if she took the rest of the afternoon off. Rats had to queue at the Post Office, fourth in a line that included an out-of-date insurance note for a motor tax renewal, a giro issued for another Post Office, a passport application and a young woman with two carrier bags full of parcels which had each to be weighed and stamped.

Walking back quickly, Rats hoped to catch the car. She was fantasising what to do when and if she saw the driver. Pretend to mistake them for a famous personality and ask for an autograph? Clutch their arm and say she'd always wanted a ride in a Rolls Royce and today was her birthday? She didn't know what she would do. Superstitiously and irrationally, she thought that to see who drove the car would make clear all the vague fears she carried around with her since first stumbling upon the body. Fears that she thought had left her but today realised were still there for her. When she reached Fortescue Avenue the car had gone. She scanned the lines of traffic moving down Mare Street. Back at the office the door was locked and Ralph was alone. He looked worried. Rats made coffee for them.

'Tell me about it,' she said.

'It's not good,' said Ralph, 'not good at all. And you're not going to like any of it.'

The office remained shut. Ralph explained to Rats that Pershing wanted to rationalise, as he put it, their end of the operation. Pershing, Ralph explained, owned a number of property related ventures. 'There's more money in bankruptcy than business these days. I think we're to be some sort of tax loss.'

'Do we really go out of business or do we just close down and open up under another name next month? That sort of deal? Or is it really going down, with a tidy pay off? And why?'

'I don't know. It's not me this time. Pershing's okay. He'll see us right. He's clever, done well for himself, you should see the car he drives. That'd give you confidence in him, you need cash on the nail for a car like that. Out of my league.'

'I'm not interested in his car, Ralph.'

Rats got up, taking their cups over to the counter. She needed something to do, to take her mind off the sudden sick realisation that she might be about to lose her job. Although she had planned to leave she had done nothing about it and doubted whether she would find another job as easily.

'As I see it, we send a letter to our tenants saying we are going into liquidation and that the properties owned by us are to be sold. At the same time, we process an application for Surefast Properties to buy out a controlling interest in the houses we own and the management agency. Then we sign contracts as employees of Surefast, change the signs and the headed notepaper and it's all hunky dory again. New contracts for us, new agreements for the tenants at only slightly higher rents, and we lose a couple of hundred thousand pounds somewhere along the way.'

'You're pretty smart, Gerry. That's about it, but you make it sound mean, sneaky. It's routine, business. It's like that in this game. If you look at it the way you do, it sounds almost illegal.'

'Oh I'm sure you're on the right side of the law. Pershing would see to that.'

'Do you want to stay? I'm going to need you, this is going to involve an awful lot of paperwork.'

'I'll stay, Ralph. I don't like it, I don't like a lot of what I'm having to do here, but I'll do it. I thought this was a pretty straight organisation but I'm beginning to think it's as crooked as hell.'

Ralph bristled. 'You don't know what you're talking about. You don't understand this business, so don't try. You can keep your pious mouthings to yourself.'

Rats shrugged. It was too familiar an argument to excite her. 'Okay, so when do we start?'

'Tomorrow,' said Ralph, 'we'll start on it tomorrow. I'm all in. It's been one hell of a today.'

They closed up and left. It was drizzling. Rats decided to walk home, she needed to clear her head, to calm herself down. Seeing the car again had unnerved her. Her tiredness, the cold wet streets, the bustle of Friday shoppers buffeted her. She felt tears prick her eyes. She needed the job, yet it unsettled her. She told herself everything had been fine until Pershing started interfering. She watched the traffic, seeing if she could spot the car. She horrified herself, acknowledging the grip of fear it held her in, her inability to understand or really ever forget it, even when it seemed she had.

The next few weeks were as busy as any Rats had known since starting to work at Lindy's. It reached a crisis level one Wednesday afternoon when Rats took a garbled phone call from Maureen. She had started to bleed and was in a panic. It was her first baby and she was in her late thirties. Rats was uneasy about Ralph driving over; he was frantic, likely to be more of a hindrance than a help. The baby was not due for a while and if Maureen was right, as she probably was, then there was a strong chance she could miscarry. It took a while for calm to settle once Ralph had gone. He promised to ring and let her know what happened, but she doubted whether he would remember until the following morning. She continued with the work, much of which she did not understand. Figures, letters full of legal jargon, phrases with a ring of solidity that evaporated when you perused them in search of meaning. Rats continued to type and file and check, licking stamp after stamp till she thought the sour, sharp taste of gum would never leave her mouth. She no longer had any sense of what sort of letters she was sending, or to whom. It became an indistinguishable labour she performed for a number of hours each day and then left.

40

At the sound of the door opening she looked up. Now that the cards had been taken out of the window and the neon sign switched off it was unlikely to be anyone in search of accommodation. Rats gritted her teeth against the inevitable oddball, the person on the scrounge with the point of view to put, the person who knew God loved them and wanted to spread the good news. But it wasn't one of these, it was Pershing.

'Ralph isn't here, I'm sorry. Anything I can do?'

'Where is he? When will he be back?'

'He went home, Maureen phoned. I don't expect him back today. If Maureen has miscarried, well, it could be a few days.'

Pershing stood looking thoughtful. 'Difficult,' he said.

Rats looked at him, feeling obliged to be helpful and resented that obligation. 'Can I help?'

'Maybe, what are you doing here right now?'

'Carrying on with some work Ralph left, filing mostly and sending out letters. When I've finished this I've nothing particular to do, just the usual, the mail and so on.'

'That's fine. I need someone to go across to Plaistow. I've an urgent job there. I would prefer Ralph but I'll have to make do with you. I'll just make a phone call.'

He went into the back where Ralph usually worked. There was the low hum of conversation. Rats couldn't distinguish the exact words but she made out that Pershing was persuading and cajoling and, finally, laying down the law. She guessed she was the subject of the persuasion – that she was definitely second best for someone.

Pershing came back through. 'That's settled then. I need someone to do some paperwork for me over at one of our hostels. The guys who run it don't take that side of things too seriously. There's a backlog to catch up on. I'll take you over tomorrow and introduce you, show you what we need doing. There's probably about ten days' work. Can you put a sign here, closed until further notice. Where exactly do you live?'

'Stoke Newington.'

'I'll pay you an extra travelling allowance while you're working at Plaistow, it's an awkward journey for you. It'll save time tomorrow if I pick you up and take you over. Say about nine? Jot your address down here will you?'

He seemed impatient to be gone. Rats hurriedly wrote out her address and gave it to him. He looked it over, then looked at her, 'Caitlin Road?' he asked unnecessarily, 'Lived there long?'

'About a year, do you know it?'

'Oh yes, I'll find my way there all right.'

Rats took advantage of the pause in his departure; she had another question for him before he went. 'Do you mean "closed until further notice"? There is going to be a job to come back to here, isn't there?'

'Anxious about your job? From what Ralph tells me I thought you'd be leaving us.' He smiled. The kind that doesn't involve your eyes. It was his usual smile and Rats didn't smile back. 'Sure there'll be a job. There are easier ways of getting rid of people than sending them to Plaistow.'

With that he left. Rats continued to sign and send her letters until the file was finished. She took the card backing off a note pad and wrote in clear, black letters: 'Closed until further notice'. Then she wrote a short note to Ralph explaining her absence. She put it to one side as she tidied the desk, cleaned the coffee area, checked the windows were locked. Then she took it through to put it on Ralph's desk.

There was another note on Ralph's desk, Rats picked it up and scanned it. It was a bad habit she had, she could never resist the urge to read other people's books, letters, diaries if they were left lying about, even people's newspapers on the bus or tube. It was simple curiosity. She saw no harm, despite the numerous times she proved the wisdom of the old saying and heard only ill of herself.

This note was written on a piece of ordinary paper, in distinctive, bold handwriting. It read: 'Ralph, things are getting difficult. A fine time for your woman to drop that brat. I had to get someone into Plaistow, it wouldn't wait for your return. I've sent that girl of yours – she's not stupid, and we need to move fast. I don't think there's any risk involved, despite what you've said. I'll be keeping an eye on her anyway. Can you pull out the stops your end when you get back? Pearsons are far from happy. Regards, Cruze.' Rats put it down, puzzled. Pearsons, she knew, were solicitors. She had had to deal with some correspondence from them a few weeks back. They had a hefty file.

There was something frightening about the note, it implied pressure and danger. She felt apprehensive, but aware of the ridiculousness of that feeling. It was only a job, their anxiety could be nothing more than a worry that she couldn't do the work they had in mind for her. Accommodation was hardly a high-risk occupation. Rats fought down the fears, not managing, however, to wholly quash them. She decided not to leave her note on Ralph's desk. It had probably not entered Pershing's head that she would go in there. For some reason she felt it important that he didn't know she had seen it. She left her note on the counter top, secured with a jar of coffee. She carried on checking the building, pulled down the shutters and locked up. As she did so, a phone began to ring inside. She let it. Straightening up from the pavement, Rats turned towards home, uneasiness settling on her.

9

The next morning Rats allowed herself plenty of time to get ready. Pershing's reference to her arguments with Ralph disturbed her; it surprised her Ralph had bothered to pass the information on. She didn't want to be late, wanted to impress Pershing, she realised, and as she closed her front door and walked across the yard, she realised too that she didn't want him ringing her bell, coming too close to where she lived. He frightened her, why she couldn't say.

Rats sat on the wall, watching the children hurrying to school, keeping an ear and an eye for Pershing. The lollipop lady stopped the cars to let a small throng of women and children over. Rats idly followed their progress to the school gates then, with a jolt, her gaze followed a car cruising the kerb, clearly looking for a particular house.

Rats watched it with a sickening fascination, willing its engine to rev and carry it past her, knowing it would, as it did, glide to a halt opposite her. She stumbled to her feet as the door opened and Pershing emerged smiling from the driver's seat of the green Rolls. He walked towards her as the school bell began to ring.

That and the children's feet flapping over the pavement were the most ominous sounds Rats could recall. She wanted to run too, or to laugh. She wanted to do anything but what she in fact did, which was to walk over to Pershing, her skin crawling, and allow him to settle her into the passenger seat of his car. She tried to control her fear, to think calmly, but her body rebelled. Her legs and hands shook, her back was drenched with sweat, her heart pounded. Pershing was watching her, a look she couldn't interpret on his face. It had no concern in it, despite him asking if she was feeling all right.

Her sense of the danger she might be in sobered her, gave her courage. She wiped the back of her hand over her face. 'I'm fine. I don't know what that was about, sorry.'

Pershing's hands were still resting on the steering wheel, he made no move to start the engine. 'Are you sure? I can take you up to your flat if you're not feeling well.'

She nodded a refusal. He started the engine, giving a thin, ironical little laugh, 'I'd hate anyone to think I was upsetting you.'

Rats was coming down from her terror, the rush of panic subsided. He's playing games with me, she thought, and wondered why. Rats, reaslising now he was the owner of the car, knew he was implicated in the death she'd witnessed. But she saw he couldn't know that. This fear played into his hands unnecessarily, gave her away. She tried to act nonchalant, giving herself time to think. 'Tell me what this job is going to involve.'

'I'm taking you to a mission, a hostel. It used to be for sailors, there was a regular turnover and the lads would pay cash in advance. These days the men are more of a mix, probably for most of them the hostel's home, they're not shipping out anywhere. And the subs are long gone. Most of them are claiming social security, a few have pensions.' Rats looked out of the window as this explanation was given. They were travelling along a kind of flyover. There were blocks of thirties' flats to her right, behind them the high rise towers. No green, no small patterned streets. It was slablike, slabs of buildings on slabs of land. There were no people and it was hard to imagine that there ever had been or ever would be. To the left, the dock wall ran between the road and the wasteland. Occasionally, she could see into the docks, their cranes standing in rows along the wharves and warehouses. The water was still, no ships disturbed its surface. It stretched for miles.

Rats was angry – at the empty spaces, the stacked houses, the easy way in which Pershing spoke of the sailors. The anger helped her deal with her fear. She closed her eyes and tried to imagine the docks working, ships tied up, being unloaded, the shore gangers with their grappling hooks dangling off their belts, steam rising from the canteen; movement, sound ringing out across the yards. Ships' hooters, voices, the sounds of machines working, cards being slapped down, a wooden box being scraped across the cobbles, whistles, fog horns. It was hard. Pershing was still speaking. She picked up the thread.

'I'll go over it with you when we get there. It's basically processing the returns on those claims, making sure that it's all in order. And while you're there you might as well check the insurance and repairs schedule and look over the books.'

They drove on in silence. Eventually, Pershing pulled up in front of a large red-bricked building. A long stone tablet across the front of the building had words etched into it. She read 'Home for Colonial Seamen 1896'. Her eyes drifted down to a smaller, painted wooden sign: 'Harry's Rooms for Hire. Night, Day, Week or Month'. Some of the windows were open, yellowed net curtains blowing in the breeze. Rats followed Pershing up the steps. As the main door jangled shut behind them a figure emerged through the door behind the reception area. A large dog of indeterminate breed roused itself from the centre of the floor and stood, ears cocked, watching them advance across the hallway.

Pershing introduced them. George had a grey, greasy pallor as if he'd been indoors too long, all his life maybe. The building smelt musty, as if air rarely penetrated. Rats hoped the job could be done quicker than Pershing thought. The atmosphere depressed her. She couldn't imagine what effect the job would have.

George lifted up the hinged flap on the desk, enabling them to follow him into the office behind. Rats almost gagged as they entered. With no windows open, ashtrays full to overflowing and more cigarettes stubbed out on the floor, the smell was sickening. There were cups covered in green mould, piles of old newspapers, betting slips, envelopes and folders. Rats assumed that this would be where she was working; she braced herself and said: 'I hope you aren't expecting me to work in here?'

George fixed her with an unpleasant look: 'We make do. There isn't anywhere else, sunshine. This or nothing.'

Pershing leaned in the doorway. 'I take the lady's point, George. It's rather squalid in here, even for this place.'

George turned his look on Pershing. 'Not your standard, Mr Pershing, I know. Can't be helped though. Our money's as good as anybody else's all the same, isn't it. Too good to waste on a place like this?'

'I'm only asking you to clean the place up a little, George, it doesn't need a song and dance.'

They found chairs and sat down. Pershing and George outlined her work. There were seventy residents, single men with no dependants. Since the introduction of housing benefit, the claim was to be made by and paid to the landlords, George and Arthur, who managed the hostel as sub-leases of another property company, Star Holdings, based in East Ham. George and Arthur had not realised they should be making any claim. It was Rats' job to pick up the claims on their behalf and to check they had accurate records of who was living in the hostel.

'Are there arrears?' asked Rats.

'No arrears, lady. Empty rooms. We take cash on the nail. These bastards would drink any amount of money, rent or no rent. We collect here.'

Rats' anger at his contempt showed in her face. But she kept quiet as Pershing continued his explanation before excusing himself, promising to drop by later to see how she was getting on. George said he'd take her on a tour round. 'Not that there's much to see.' She followed him back into the reception area.

'There's nobody about now, we don't encourage residents to stay here during the day. Out by eight-thirty, doors open again at seven, locked at midnight.'

Rats said nothing, her face gave her away.

'You should get to know a few before you start wearing your heart on your sleeve for them. They're looked after.' He moved towards a door. 'The rooms are off the staircases through these doors. The dining room is here to the right and the kitchen is beyond that.'

They walked into the dining room. It had long trestle tables and benches and the tables were set for a meal in a rudimentary fashion. A sweet stale smell reminiscent of school meals but much, much older pervaded the room. Rats was drawn by the two statues in the room, both old, worn smooth. Religious. The sacred heart poured out its plaster life blood, reaching an imploring hand into the void. The mother and child gazed into each other's faces, oblivious to the motherless men who would later be herded below them, some still making a mumbled grace before their meals.

George led the way into the kitchen. It was steamy, the smells of food strong and pleasant. Huge pots bubbled on the stove, a cook was placing a pastry cover on a large pie.

'Arthur, this is Gerry. Pershing sent her along to help out with the claims.'

'Hello Arthur,' said Rats, hoping for an ally against George.

46

'Showing you round is he love? Well, this is the only place you need to know about. Pot of tea anytime you fancy, and none of our guests ever sets foot in the place. I do all my own washing up.' He was smiling, his manner was less imposing than George's, but his sentiments were the same, however pleasantly expressed to her. Tea was produced and they drank and talked. Rats found herself asking them questions about Pershing. They answered them, George gruffly and with some reluctance, Arthur with relish, giving all the signs of loving to gossip.

His mannerisms were exaggerated, camp even. He was chatting to her now about Pershing, how they'd first met, how they'd come to work for him. His little foibles, how to humour him.

George was irritated by this line of conversation. 'You're very interested in Pershing. Got your eye on him, have you? I wouldn't waste my time. You're not in his league.'

Arthur started to giggle until George silenced him with a stiff look.

Rats was hurt by the remark and Arthur's laughter. Arthur was sensitive to that and gave her a broad grin. 'Nothing personal. It's a private joke, Pershing's ladies. You mustn't breathe a word about it. Not a word to anyone. No offence. George doesn't appreciate women, do you?'

George's response was to head out of the kitchen, pausing at the door. 'Pershing isn't paying you to drink tea all day. Either of you.'

Back in the small office, George had found a plastic waste paper bin, a dust pan, a brush and a duster. He had no intention of using them, but handed them to Rats. He went and sat in the reception area with a pile of paper and betting slips. Yesterday's losers. Rats began to clean up the office, emptying ashtrays and sweeping the butts up from the floor. The dirty cups and mugs she took through to the kitchen, but didn't stop to chat with Arthur; he was busy and she didn't want to risk more of George's ill humour. Finally, she cleared a space for herself to work at the table. George chain smoked, muttering to himself as one after another the betting slips were torn up and thrown away.

Rats started to make a list from the files in the cabinets. They were a brief, eloquent record of everyday tragedy, containing the barest details of the men's lives. Most of them were in their fifties, some younger, some older. They were all, bar three or four, unemployed. Their trades were those of casual labour, they had no next of kin, save occasional addresses in the west of Ireland or the north of Scotland.

From time to time the forms would not be signed, just marked with a clumsy cross. Rats speculated on the circumstances that brought the men to this place, wondered if she would ever meet them. There must be places like this for women too. She tried to imagine what it would be like to call this place home. She imagined that under these circumstances you don't call any place home.

She decided to phone the DHSS to try and clarify the procedure for making a claim. It took forty minutes to get through, then a further ten to find someone who could help her. Finally, they suggested an appointment. Rats wondered whether George should go, George shook his head. Rats took her hand off the mouthpiece and made a note of the appointment, three-thirty that afternoon. To fill in time Rats looked over the books. They all seemed to be in order.

George leaned his head around the door. 'Arthur'll have dinner for us in about fifteen minutes. Then you can go out to the benefit office. It'll take all afternoon. Make sure you know how to get here in the morning before you go. You won't be getting a lift every day.'
He went back to his paper and disappeared out of the door with a list of hopefuls for the afternoon's racing.

Rats stood in the foyer. Her curiosity about the living quarters got the better of her. On the first floor a corridor opened off each side of the landing. She followed one, there was a sharp smell in the air, a mixture of sweat, damp clothes, stale urine and an indefinable smell that was, she supposed, simply humanity. Each of the doors opened out into a large dormitory, partitioned off to form six cubicles. In each cubicle was a single bed, made up, a bedside table, a rail for clothes which ran along one side of the partition; on the other side men had either stuck photos, scrawled messages or left them blank. A cut out page three girl, the odd religious card, personal photographs, faded with age. In one, a model ship worked in matchsticks, a personal glass and ashtray. In another a special bed cover. Rats found herself walking on tiptoe, holding her breath. She felt as if she was trespassing. As she came through the doors into the hall she encountered George.

'Had a good nose round, love? Interesting, was it?'

'I was looking for the toilet. Still am.'

'Over there, where it says "toilets".' He gestured dismissively after her and went through into the dining room.

Rats followed shortly, obliged first to carry through the pretence of needing the toilet. She sat down while Arthur doled out portions of a meat pie, cabbage and potatoes. There was no conversation until they finished. Arthur went out to make tea and George lit a cigarette in the same movement as he pushed away his plate. Rats felt awkward, glanced around the room, but there was little to look at. She traced the initials carved into the table with her finger. Arthur returned with the tea things.

'Nice to have a new face,' he said, settling down expectantly opposite Rats. He poured tea for the three of them.

'What do you do all day?' Rats asked.

'Questions, questions. What are you? The bleeding Spanish Inquisition?' George snarled and stormed out of the room, leaving his tea untouched.

Arthur flinched at his words, his hands went nervously to his face, smoothing his hair down. Then he picked up his tea and put it down again. Rats sat feeling foolish, unsure what to do. It seemed there was no correct way for her to behave, she rubbed George up the wrong way everyway.

'You shouldn't take it to heart. He's got a wicked temper, but he's a lovely bloke, one of the best. I should know.'

'I'm sure he is. I just wish he'd get off my back. I don't enjoy being here anymore than he likes it. Why can't we just make the best of it?'

'I'll have a word with him later.'

Rats finished her tea, collected instructions on how to find the place again and left to keep her appointment with the DHSS. She said goodbye to George as she went through the hallway. He grunted at her.

10

It didn't take long to find the DHSS office. It was crowded, so she had to wait, of course, and it took her some while to establish exactly where she should be waiting. The interview, when it came, was perfunctory. She was handed forms, told to be sure to get signatures and asked to return them as soon as possible.

As she walked back along the cubicles she could hear voices raised, always the claimant's, and was struck by the reasonableness of what she heard. In the waiting room, there seemed to be even more people. There was a deflated air to the room, unalleviated by the restless playing up of the children, the small conversation groups the young people formed. Rats went down the stairs, relieved that she had, for all its problems, a job to go to tomorrow.

Rats caught a train home, it ran overground beside the River Lea and the canal. There was a view, fleetingly, into the back yards and windows of countless lives. She caught the bus up from Dalston, feeling exhausted, desperate to get home and collapse on her bed.

Once there, her attempt to relax only increased her fear. She felt again the clumsy outline of her body against the smooth, leather upholstery which had also cradled that mutilated corpse. She dozed off, found herself driven, recklessly, by Pershing, in a car so splattered with blood that they couldn't see out of the windows. George's voice echoed inside her head. What it was saying she couldn't grasp. She started awake, her heart pounding. Awake, she brooded on the tangible problems of her job and found that plenty to be going on with. She looked at her watch, it was nine o'clock. Brenda ought to be back in town now. It would be a relief to see her, a connection back to her life before the job, before the body. Rats decided to walk round and see if she wanted to go out for a drink. Something had to take away the taste of the day.

Rats had known Brenda almost as long as she'd been in London. Their friendship had weathered the extremes of Rats' despair. Brenda, considerably older than Rats, exerted a calming influence on her. She tried to make sure Rats ate properly and looked after herself; she nagged her incessantly about her drinking. It was Brenda who made sure they kept in touch, often difficult when Rats was low.

When Rats first moved to London she had made various attempts to meet other women, mainly scouring the gay section in a listings magazine. She dutifully went to the groups and meetings that were reasonably central and made a note of the bars. On the whole she found the meetings frustrating, turning up to some odd discussions, simply because they had the word 'Lesbian' in them somewhere. She, like others, went not so much for the issue as for the lesbianism. But it never seemed appropriate to mention it. She knew the inclusive matiness was well meant, and she appreciated it. But all the same, it made her tongue-tied and clumsy. The bars were a different matter all together. Usually she spent the night propping the wall up, too shy and intimidated by the other women, who all seemed to know each other, to make any kind of move towards them. The only exceptions were the nights when Dutch courage rendered her noisily ebullient, drunk and irresponsible. They were the nights she would rather forget.

She had been sitting one evening while a discussion went over her head when she realised a woman sitting opposite her was trying to catch her eye, pulling a 'what are we doing here?' face. Rats smiled back. At the inevitable break, where those who knew each other went into huddles and those that didn't competed to make the coffee, to have something useful to do, Rats walked over to Brenda. She looked vaguely familiar; as it turned out, they both lived in the same area. They decided to go for a drink and turned their backs forever on Lesbianism: An Issue for Christianity. Brenda had gone to the meeting, as she put it, out of a sense of nostalgia. Brought up in a staunch Methodist family, she had broken all ties with them ten years ago when they had supported her ex-husband in the custody case she lost. Her mother's death the previous year had led Brenda to reconsider her childhood and its strong religious influence. She thought the meeting might provide a way to connect back. It hadn't.

They exchanged stories over drinks and from there a friendship developed. Rats came to rely on Brenda for companionship and guidance. Brenda enjoyed being involved with a younger woman who admired her experience and let herself be mothered, in a low-key sort of way. Rats appreciated the solid, quiet way Brenda lived her life, uncompromisingly lesbian, but only slightly involved in the politics or club land of the city.

As Rats set off that evening she argued with herself about how much to tell Brenda. Approaching her house, Rats tried to sort out what she was going to say. As she rehearsed it in her head, the ludicrousness competed with the horror. It sounded exaggerated, paranoid. There was the body, her job, some kind of connection between them. The desire to share her fear, and by so doing have it lessened, wasn't strong enough to overcome her unwillingness to expose even more vulnerability. Brenda, too, would make much of her having been drunk the night she found the body. Rats remembered just how drunk she had been, and a nagging doubt about the reality of the whole incident still ate away at her. Until she had more to tell, she would stay silent; concentrate on the positive changes since she'd last seen Brenda. She had a job now, mostly life felt calmer and as for the body, well she hoped she could, eventually, forget.

Brenda came to the door and they set out for the pub, talking generally about their lives, their jobs. Rats gossiped about George, Arthur and the hostel. It was Brenda who said, 'Sounds rum, that set up. You want to watch out for yourself. I don't like the sound of any of them,' as the saloon bar swung shut behind them.

The following day, George was no easier a workmate. Settled with his paper and betting slips, he barely nodded a response to her 'good morning'. From time to time she had to consult him: he gave her whatever information she asked for and returned to his study of form. At half-past eleven George disappeared to return with tea for himself and Rats. Shortly afterwards the phone rang: George answered it and passed the receiver over to Rats. It was Ralph. Maureen was in hospital, the panic seemed to be over, but they were taking no chances. He was going to be in the office on Friday and wanted her to call in then. She checked with George who responded with a shrug of the shoulders that she should please herself.

Rats worked steadily, it was not an arduous task, fiddly but the sort of thing it was possible to progress with fairly quickly. Lunchtimes were a pleasant break; Arthur seemed as starved of conversation as she was and Rats had no problem in keeping Pershing as their main topic of discussion. George rarely joined in and when he did it was rather sourly to check their curiosity about Pershing.

On Thursday they sat over their tea with Arthur in full flight and Rats feeding him questions to gently keep him to the point. Her point, Pershing. Recalling the incident, Rats remembered George smiling to himself, an unusual occurrence. But then, he faced the door Arthur and Rats had their backs to.

'I thought my ears were burning. What is it now? Left for spite?' Pershing moved into the room, joining them at the table but remained standing up. George smiled in a self-satisfied way at Rats.

'Here he is, why don't you ask him directly whatever it is you want to know about him. Then perhaps we can all have our meals in peace.' He turned to Pershing, 'Sit down, Mr Pershing, Arthur'll fetch you a cup. You're causing quite a stir in our young lady here, she doesn't seem to have a thought in her head that isn't for you.'

Arthur shot up from the table relieved to be doing something. He bustled about Pershing seeing whether he had eaten, if he wanted tea or coffee. Pershing watched Rats, waiting for her to speak.

'What's all the fuss about? Arthur and I don't exactly have a lot else to talk about do we?'

Pershing smiled as he sat down across from Rats. 'No fuss at all, depending of course on what you were saying.' He waited. Rats said nothing more. George filled him in.

Leaning across towards Rats, Pershing stared at her a moment or two before he spoke. 'I would have thought a girl like you had better things to occupy herself with. It isn't a very healthy interest and I don't see quite where you think it might lead you. It's really none of your business, you know, any of it. It doesn't flatter me, Miss Flannagan, to know you take such an interest in me and my affairs. On the contrary.'

He took a mouthful of his coffee and swallowed it with a pained expression. 'It leaves a nasty taste, almost as bad as the coffee, eh?' He slapped George on the back, grinning, inviting George and Arthur to laugh with him, at themselves, and stood up.

'That was all very interesting, but it wasn't what I came over for. I want a word with both of you, in the office.'

Rats stayed where she was, brooding on the exchange. It all felt more serious that it warranted. She felt warned off, Pershing had spoken calmly, reasonably even, but something else lurked behind his words. George and Arthur returned about twenty minutes later. Arthur smiled, a little bashfully, George simply told her to get back to work. Rats was relieved to be going into the office tomorrow, looked forward to seeing Ralph.

Ralph wasn't there when Rats got to the office the following morning. She waited a bit, hands in pockets, then walked slowly up and down the pavement. Ralph arrived just gone ten; he was unshaven and his clothes had a crumpled look. Rats saw him from a distance and quickened her pace. She had a surge of warm feeling, wanted to rush up and fling her arms around him. Instead, she realised that he had probably not remembered to bring fresh milk in with him. She turned into a newsagents and bought milk, coffee and sugar. She satisfied her impulsive fellow feeling by buying a packet of Jaffacakes.

'How's everything? It's good to see you, how's Maureen?'

He was preoccupied, took the packages from her and set about filling the kettle. 'Fine, fine. It's me that's the problem. Christ knows how I fared for myself before I met Maureen. I don't know whether I'm coming or going.'

Rats smiled at his bemused face. She wondered whether Maureen was as appreciated when she was around as she was in her absence. Ralph's gesture of hospitality extended only as far as filling the kettle and switching it on. Rats, in her relief at not having to confront George that morning, was prepared to let it ride. She made the coffee, opened the biscuits and sat down.

'How are you finding the hostel?'

'Pretty grim. The work's easy enough, but I don't like the bloke at all.'

'The bloke? Two of them there I thought, or have they had a tiff?' Ralph laughed, a snickering sort of laugh.

'There are two. Arthur's all right. It's George I can't stand.'

'You don't need to worry. Bent, they are.' He leered suggestively, 'Needn't waste your feminine charm on that pair.'

Rats wished she hadn't spoken, wondered why she thought there might have been a bit of sympathy in the offing from Ralph. He seemed to enjoy upsetting her.

'That doesn't worry me. He's not a nice bloke. Who he sleeps with has nothing to do with it.'

'Another crusade for you there. Sorry I spoke.'

All her conversations with Ralph seemed to lead to conflict. Rats let it slide. 'Another job,' she told herself, 'forget it, leave it alone.' Her rosy expectations of the morning were fading. It was as bad here as it had been at Plaistow or would be at home. All around, the colour of grey settled down.

'What did you want to see me about, Ralph? I'm still busy over in Plaistow.'

'I need to find my way around these files. I don't quite see how you've been doing it.' He indicated the files stacked on the desk, just as she had left them.

'Can't you just leave them for me? I can finish it off when I'm done at the hostel. It's not going to take that long to sort out their problems.'

'Well, we could, yeah. It's just that Pershing wants it done quickly you know and, er . . . ' He tailed off, looking at his hands.

'I don't know Ralph, if it can wait three or four days I'll do it. If not, it'll take a couple of hours to show you how to do it properly.'

'You'd better show me.'

Rats started to gather her pieces of work together, setting them out so as to show Ralph how to carry on the work she'd begun. 'Have you known Pershing long? Funny sort of bloke I think.'

'In what way? He's sound, Pershing is, sound as a bell. I've known him years. Like that, we are.' Ralph clasped his forefingers together and held them briefly in front of Rats. 'Nothing he wouldn't do to help a friend.'

'Well set up, isn't he? He gave me a lift over in that car of his. Lovely it was.'

Ralph sighed appreciatively. 'Yeah, what a car. But he's no airs about him, doesn't come it the big boss man.'

'But he is the big boss man, isn't he?'

'Of course he is, definitely. More fingers in more pies than a cook'd know what to do with. But he doesn't put it over on you. He's all right.'

'Is it all legit, what he's into? On the level?'

Ralph lost his dreamy look. 'On the level? What're you on about? Watching too much telly. You've just got it in for anybody with the sense to make something of themselves. You haven't got what it takes yourself, so you take it out on all those that have. You ain't half nosey. At least Maureen was only ever interested in his women.'

'More than one has he?'

'None of your business, is it?'

Ralph picked up the file nearest to him. 'Let's get on with this, shall we?' He dangled it in front of her face, 'Work.'

It took Rats a fair while to go through the systems with Ralph. It was straightforward enough, but he was slow on the uptake. There was little opportunity to talk, but when there was, Rats kept plugging away at Pershing. Since seeing Brenda again the need to tell what had happened clamoured in Rats' mind. But as the need grew, so did the belief that she would need to know more before speaking to Brenda or anyone. She needed something tangible to tell her, something outside herself. So she set herself to find out as much as she could about Pershing. His work, his business, his women, where he lived, where he'd come from.

Ralph was cautious and non-committal, he didn't have a flair for gossip, but just occasionally he'd run away with himself, get caught up in his story. A picture began to emerge for Rats of Pershing, partly from what she'd seen of him, partly from what Ralph and others let slip. Everything she did learn about Pershing confirmed him as a menacing, powerful figure, especially his reaction to her yesterday. Rats imagined gangland warfare, shady business deals, death. Some of it, naturally, she could only speculate upon. As she worked, her mind ostensibly on the job in hand, she was piling up fragments, hoping that they would eventually form a whole. The picture she wanted was the one that was going to tell her who it was who was dead, slumped in Pershing's car and why it was his car that carried such a cargo.

He was something of a womaniser, lacking a basic understanding of how to please and be pleased by women. After three marriages, he was now alone, but never short of female company. Ralph had a piece of scandal to pass on, he relished the telling of this, less for the content than for the impression it gave that he and Pershing were the sort to confide in each other, man to man. Earlier that year, Ralph thought he recognised a girlfriend of Pershing's in a newspaper article. The woman had committed suicide. When asked, Pershing confirmed it was her, but that he had stopped seeing her a few weeks before the incident. Pershing wasn't mentioned in the paper, but another boyfriend was and he concluded that she must have been two-timing him.

'Scheming little madam, I'm better off without her,' Pershing had forcibly maintained. And Ralph, remembering the depth of Pershing's infatuation, had felt it wiser not to contradict him.

It was a confidence between the two of them, Pershing insisted, man to man. Ralph agreed to tell no one, not even Maureen. 'After all, like he says, women can't keep a secret. They don't know the meaning of the word. It could cause him a lot of aggravation to be mixed up with that death.'

Rats was surprised this had all happened so recently, Pershing did not give the impression of having suffered anything out of the ordinary.

Rats turned over what she now knew of him, from Ralph and Arthur as well as from her own observations. His house in Epping had a low voltage electrical fence circling the limits of its extensive grounds. It was rumoured that dogs ran loose but Ralph had never seen them. The house had impressed Ralph with its elegant comfort, its luxury.

Pershing had an interest in a great number and variety of businesses. A kind of controlling directorship, but at one, sometimes two or three removes, with offices in Hackney and in Kensington. He travelled and was very, very wealthy. Ralph knew or revealed little of his origins.

The more she thought about him the more uncomfortable it made her. She was scared of Pershing, all the fear contained in that short encounter with death on a dark dripping street reformed in the smooth lines of the car and finally took on the lines and angles of Pershing's face.

By lunchtime, Ralph was beginning to get the hang of the system. Once he did understand it, he was contemptuous, making out it was the very simplicity of what he had to do that had eluded him. Rats smiled to herself, typical bloody man, she thought. Ralph seemed to have rubbed off some of his sharp edges. When he suggested lunch at a nearby pub, Rats was only too happy to accept. It delayed her return to Plaistow. Before they left the office, Ralph put through a call. She heard him make excuses into the phone, pausing before someone's bad temper and slowly, all over again, making his explanations. She pricked up her ears when she heard him say, 'You can have her back on Monday.' When he finished he turned to her, 'Afternoon off for you. You don't tell and I won't, okay?'

'Thanks a lot,' said Rats, following him out the door. Ralph didn't tell her that George's ill humour was partly because there were two men at Plaistow wanting to see her. They went their separate ways after lunch. The men were waiting for Ralph when he returned. They came inside and questioned him as to Rats' whereabouts. Rats recognised the men as Pershing's handymen. Ralph had done business with them a few times, when he'd needed properties emptying or had problems with squatters. He was surprised they had any business with Rats and, momentarily, he worried for her.

11

The last few days had been difficult. Rats decided to try and walk off some of the anxiety and fear. Abney Park, the old cemetery, was a place of calm contemplation for her. Today, all this week, the world seemed nothing more than a pile of ashes and a dirty taste in the mouth. It had lost its tones and half tones, everything that sparkles or glows, hums along, in harmony with itself.

Rats walked slowly down the broad avenue. Coming here was acquiring the same ritual that Mass going once had. A place you went to with invisible boundaries, where you left something behind, adopted an attitude, a bearing. Mass she remembered as noise. The congregation swelling the church with Aves and Amens, responses, the mystery of Latin, here the only sounds were her relentless thoughts, arguing with herself. What was real, what was safe. Far above her was the sound of bird song.

In amongst the dead, she found a kind of peace, not to sit and contemplate, or a peace she could describe. But it soothed her to walk in the cemetery, to push her way through the tangled paths that cut across it, made by people tending graves and memories of the dead or seeking seclusion with a loved one. How public these acts of private worship became, there for the idle gaze of the passer-by, the plastic flowers, the silver foil cut-out 'MUM', the discarded Durex, the grass crumpled from the pressure of kneeling, in an act of sorrowing or sexuality.

As a child Rats had played in cemeteries, unaware of death. The cemetery had been a wilderness playground, better than the park where the keepers nagged you off the grass and out of the trees, limiting the promised space and freedom. There caution was the glimpse of a hearse moving slowly through the gates, people leaning in against each other as they walked from the small chapel to the hole, freshly dug with the planks balanced across it, wide and deep.

Rats had collected chips of gravel from the graves, taken them home and made patterns in the backyard. Names fallen out of common use fascinated her. And she collected poems, inscriptions that rattled round her head, chants to evoke even now the scents and textures of herself as a child. Grown up, she still found the grave stones irresistible, though she was cautious about being seen to linger. The cemetery was a wild, unkempt place. The dignified sweep of its entrance was soon lost to the tangled gravestones, heaped anyhow to clear space for the freshly dug, black earth mounds marked by fresh wreaths. Mimosa filled the air with a sweet heavy fragrance that hung uneasily over this fresh evidence of death. From the neat, tended lawn with appropriate borders depending on the season: snowdrops in February, crocuses in March, daffodils in April, now primulas, pansies, snap dragons, wallflowers. The cemetery stretched back, a tangle of brambles, trees and grasses. Vegetation flourished here, away from the snip and chop of the planner, a breathing space from the leaden air of the main roads, nourished on centuries of the dead.

There was a moment when the sky was simply sky, bright and clear. When the grass, flowers and headstones were simply there. But then the sky seemed to shift, blanketing out the light and wrapping Rats in a dark, uneasy world. It was the sound of the feet behind her, matching her own. The light hadn't changed. Her thoughts had rarely left Pershing, that car, the death. Rats was scared and in her mood wary of the people around her, nervous of the world. In her agitated state, she believed the people behind her were not casual visitors to the graveyard. They were people with intent and she was that intent. Each path looked much like the others, none offered itself as immediately obvious as the escape route through to the street and people. Each path led deeper into the tangle of bramble and bush. Rats quickened her pace. At a point neither better nor worse for it, she began to run, conscious that she was acknowledging pursuit. Something suggested stopping and turning round, facing her hunters and attempting to walk past in the opposite direction. As she ran, she felt how desperate her situation was. The men had to be linked to the events of the last few months. She was unused to, and ungainly in her flight, safety seemed always just out of reach, hidden in the last curve of the path. The men, she realised, did not need the menace of Pershing. As men pursuing a woman in a deserted place, they had enough of their own.

She saw the hands as she felt them close on her, stopped by the pressure of them.

'Hey girl, easy now.'

The face had a mouth, it was moving. Words were coming out. She could hear that.

'Hey girl, easy now.'

The face was clean shaven, an oddity above the massed layers of grubby, grimy clothing. It was the face of an older man, breaking her flight but only just checking the panic of that desperate hurling onwards. She looked the face square on. It looked back.

He released his grip on her forearms, held her hands and pulled her gently forward. They were standing by the grave of William Booth, founder of the Salvation Army. A massive, granite rebuke to the world of materialism, it seemed to rise above the squalor of the lager cans and cider bottles that littered the bench opposite it. Rats took it in with a long, lingering gaze that lodged in her mind as possibly her last. Drunks toasting each other across from the grave of that dedicated teetotaller.

The hands that pulled her were gentle, the eyes that tried to hold her own were concerned. Footsteps echoed in her heart as she allowed herself to be led behind this monument of a grave in amongst the other, lesser graves, between the arches of the bushes and through the grass. They stopped in an area no different to her from any other she knew. The man pulled away two grave slabs, the writing faded to fractions of words. Doing so revealed black plastic sheeting, weighted with stones. Removing these, he unfurled the sheet to form an entrance. He beckoned her inside.

Rats watched these preparations with resignation. She no longer trusted the world around her, anything now could happen. Her mind was full of images of resurrection. Of the stone being rolled back, of the cave that was both defeat and triumph, of the memory of women ministering with myrhh, bandages and palms. Her upbringing visioned a Gethsemane, redemption.

She walked into the cave. It was just possible to stand up in it. Cardboard boxes had been flattened and used to cover the floor. There were wooden packing cases, draped with material and a construction of bricks used as a fireplace. In the left hand area as they stood looking in, a small grotto had been put together. Pieces of glass, silk, plastic and real flowers, scraps of silver and coloured foil paper were arranged to complement each other. There was a plastic container with water in it, a billy can with the enamel flaked off in patches, a plate, some cups and a large pile of newspaper.

The man walked Rats the few feet from the entrance to one of the packing cases. He motioned for her to sit, which she did, gripping the sides of the case. He brought out a blanket, checked and woollen, bobbled with age and matted with a fine layer of dirt. He wrapped it around her shoulders and brought the two ends up across her legs, crossing them over and laying them on her lap as he did so. With the action, reminiscent of childhood, she realised that she was shaking all over and that, had she anything to say, her voice would be silenced by its tremors. He watched her from the other packing case. 'I'm not lighting up for tea. Don't know where they be now. Don't risk it girl, not for tea. You can manage without for a while.' Rats nodded. She thought she smiled, she meant to, but her face was as rigid in its fear as her other muscles were jumpy. Minutes passed.

She was conscious of the musty smell of dirt and the clean, sharp smell of earth, the warmth hemmed in by cold, damp air. The cave was dark, some light found its way through the cracks between the slabs of stone, but the general atmosphere was of dimness. The man sat and watched Rats for a while, he did not speak to her, but his lips moved and a low rush of words, too subtle for hearing, engaged him. After some time, he rose and brought out two candles, fixed on to the bottom of half-pint beer glasses. He lit these and they cast a sallow light into the cave.

'They'm gone now, I can feel the ease again. You know things like that, living this way. You can feel the pressure and the watching.'

Rats realised, slowly coming back to her body, that she had been expecting this man to be drunk. But there was no alcohol on his breath and this refuge was not a drinkers' den. There was a serenity, a gentleness about this man as out of place as the neatness of this rough shelter, his own clean face and hands. Rats felt her everyday distrust of men slide away in the face of these odd happenings.

'They was after you, wasn't they? It happens in this place, men coming after girls. But they was two, wasn't they? And they was after you. Sometimes I just come out and stand, it scares them off. Other times I has to do more. This time they was most definitely after you.'

'They were,' said Rats, 'they were definitely after me. I don't know them, though. Do you?'

'I don't know many folk. I keep myself to myself. But I don't like to see harm done. If I can do that, I do, keep people from harm. But I keeps myself to myself. We can have tea now. You'd like some tea, wouldn't you, girl?'

Rats wanted tea. Wanted the everyday occurrence that taking tea meant. She nodded. Her throat alternately dried and flooded with saliva, her fear abating and rushing back at her. Conscious that she had been rescued, though unsure from what, she registered her fear. That the rescue was another trap, not knowing who or what to trust, even her own reactions.

'Who are you?'

'My own man, girl, my own man I am.'

He handed her tea to her as he spoke and she took it gratefully. The silence was broken by the sound of a hand bell. Rats started, confused for a moment as to where she was. The rhythmic clanging could have been a school bell. The man stood up.

'Time to go girl. They're closing up for the night.'

He held a hand out to her. She stood up and he led her gently back to the side gate saying nothing more as they walked or even when he took his leave of her, turning back the way they'd come.

12

It went from bad to worse at Plaistow. She had to work too closely with George to be able to shrug off his hostility towards her. She needed signatures for the forms as she completed them. He was sullen, but argumentative, he needled her over everything from how she dressed to how she spoke, took every opportunity to accuse her of slack work, going back to the day Mr Pershing had wanted her and she couldn't be found at work. Her accent was a constant source of amusement, mimicked whenever she spoke to him.

The following Thursday when Pershing called by to check their progress the atmosphere was thick enough to slice. Pershing was pleasant enough with her, then he and George went through into the dining room. Rats had almost completed her tasks. She was setting out the procedure to be followed when any new resident was taken in when Pershing reappeared alone. Rats looked up.

'Almost finished?'

'Yes. I should have it done tomorrow. Do you want to look it over?'

'No, I'm sure you've done it very thoroughly. You'll be glad to be going, won't you?'

'Yes, its a long journey here and I've not been made exactly welcome.'

'It takes two to argue.'

'It's not about arguing. It's about being uncomfortable, made to feel in the way.'

'Perhaps you were – are.'

Rats wondered why she brought out the worst in people. 'I'll be glad to get back to Mare Street and Ralph.'

'I wanted to talk to you about that. I'd have preferred Ralph to see you, but it doesn't seem worth it when I can tell you now. That job's finished too. There's nothing there for you. We'll be finishing you tomorrow, you can pick up your cards in the morning, then come on over to wind things up here.'

'You're sacking me?'

'Not exactly sacking. The job's over, redundancy really. We just don't need you anymore.'

'You've got other places, you could fit me in somewhere.'

'I'm sure I don't need to tell you about the job situation. You take such an interest in things, I'm sure you are familiar with the latest unemployment figures.'

Rats felt tears in her eyes. It was important not to shed them now, in front of this man.

'We'll be paying you in lieu of notice.'

There was nothing more to say to him. He paused, gave a shrug and was gone. By the time George reappeared Rats had her emotions under control. She felt bitter, and puzzled. There had been no talk of Ralph's business ceasing trading for good. She felt eased out, perhaps some rumour had gone back to him. She never had found out why he had sent his men looking for her, here and at Mare Street. Perhaps she'd gone too far, trying to find out about him, made her doubts and suspicions about him too apparent. She felt scared, angry and just a little desperate.

The rest of the afternoon passed in a haze. On the way home, Rats bought a quarter bottle of whiskey, the first since she'd been working. At home she drank it, getting slowly and quietly drunk. As she did so she muttered out loud some of her anger and bitterness, shed tears for herself. She was a good worker, they had all said so. She didn't believe in the redundancy, she had been sacked.

She tried to unravel the reasons why. The rows with Ralph seemed possible but it seemed that they had patched that up. Maybe it had rankled deeper than he let on, perhaps his geniality the other day had been a way of making his subsequent actions all the more hurtful. Rats doubted this. His anger was like his personality, sharp and quick to come to the rise, then finished. Anyway, thought Rats, with the heat and impetuosity of the whiskey in her, I'll have it out with him tomorrow. Other possibilities eluded Rats, she would glimpse them then watch them slip to the edges of her mind. She drank more whiskey in an attempt to pin them down, but all it did was float them further out of reach.

The incident in Abney Park came back to her; it seemed linked, hadn't Pershing sent a couple of his men round to find her? They couldn't have wanted her for anything to do with work. It had to be linked to Pershing in a more personal way. This fear and absence of control combined with the drink to make her maudlin, overwhelmed her with self-pity. She found herself sobbing, engulfed by the need for arms to hold her, a shoulder to push her fuddled aching head into. She named the absence as Helen who would understand, give her strength. The naming served only to distress her further. A phrase of Pershing's came back, 'taking an interest'. Perhaps she had been too eager to question people about him. He might have been irritated at her intrusion, but there must have been more to it than that. Things seemed to go wrong for her since he had been around. She remembered saying to him that she had seen his car around, wondered whose it was. But he had asked her when and where, and then when he knew where she lived something seemed to change. She could not believe he did not know about the body in his car. Perhaps he suspected she knew about it too.

At the stage of drunken despair she had reached it seemed obvious Pershing was behind it all. It was the only explanation. She took herself to bed, the last glass undrunk on her beside table, the sidelight on, the radio whistling its tune-out signal and the cat waiting patiently on the wrong side of the front door.

She woke early the next day with a throbbing headache. Fumbling for the kitchen light and kettle socket, she made coffee, swallowed two large glasses of orange juice and two aspirin. She went down to let her cat in and stood enjoying the grey-blue peacefulness of the early morning as he rushed gratefully towards her. She went back to bed and lay, sipping coffee and stroking the cat, thinking about her suddenly diminished future.

She dozed off again, woke later, got up and dressed. She didn't relish having to confront Ralph, but felt she must, she might even persuade him to let her stay on. When she reached the office, Ralph was already there. He didn't offer her coffee.

'What's all this about, Ralph? Are you sacking me?'

'Sorry, Gerry, but you know what was happening here. There's not going to be a job. I'm sorry. It's nothing personal, I'm sure of that. I was worried the other week when those fellas were here for you, they'd already been to Plaistow. But I squared it with Pershing, I told him I made you take the afternoon off. It wasn't that.'

'Ralph, I don't understand. I've worked well, here and in Plaistow. I don't see what I've done to deserve the sack. It's not right.'

'It's not like that. There's no job. Your sort of person . . .' Ralph's voice rose and fell. 'You're never satisfied, never see things the way they are. The job's finished, that's all there is to it.'

Rats watched Ralph looking uncomfortable. She was not going to get any joy here. Ralph handed her an envelope. It contained her P45 and a wad of notes.

'That's it then,' she said, taking it off him.

'I am sorry Gerry, really. If anything comes up I'll be in touch. Look in on us when the baby's born, eh? Maureen'd like to see you again.'

'Sure, yeah,' said Rats, opening the door onto the street, 'I'll see you around.'

As Rats went across the road to study the bus routes to Plaistow she wondered why she was bothering to go. She'd more or less finished, she'd been paid off, she didn't owe them anything. But her own values asserted themselves, those forged in the heart of the family. 'If a job's worth doing' rang in her head, speaking with her mother's voice as she started to clean the steps, again. Nothing in her upbringing would allow her to walk away, still owing a day's work, however deep her contempt for the boss.

If George and Arthur knew about the loss of her job they didn't let on. The day passed, similar to the others she'd spent there. At five she left, said goodbye to them both and made her way to the railway station. She had not, in the two weeks she'd been there, seen or heard any trace of the residents. They were names, on forms, in files. They would fade.

She didn't have to wait long for a train. The compartment she got into was not very crowded. Sitting across from two women, Rats found herself watching them. The younger of the two radiated energy, drew attention. She had an astonishing head of ginger hair, long and thick, but soft at the same time. Rats had an urge to reach across and touch it. She wore a short, tight green dress, fashionable but cheap. She was giggly, talking with the other woman. They passed notebooks back and forth, seemed to be discussing a class of some sort. Rats assumed they were students, envied their lives, their freedom to giggle with each other on a Friday afternoon.

The older woman, about thirty, was trying to persuade the other to give her a cigarette. 'No, you've given up. You can't give up and still

65

smoke. No.' She spoke with an authority at variance to her appearance and attitude. The older woman reached for the packet, the younger passed it from hand to hand out of her reach. Finally, the older woman sat back defeated. There was a pause, then a fresh burst of giggles, snorts and drawing of breath. The woman with the cigarette had no matches, the other woman had produced a box and passed it from her hands, one to another, mimicking her friend's performance with the cigarettes. Her friend took the cigarette out of her mouth and threw it at her.

'There you are, you cow.'

'Bitch.'

The cigarette hit Rats' shoulder and fell to the floor. She bent down to pick it up and passed it to the woman on her right. Both were doubled up, tears streaming down their faces. One or two people in the carriage flicked their papers down, a few moved their seats. One small boy stood staring, fascinated despite his mother's attempts to tug him into a seat. Rats, irrational though she knew the thought to be, felt the laughter directed against her.

They drew in and out of maybe four stations. People got on and off at each one. Rats looked up at the women who had suddenly gone very quiet. She followed their gaze out of the window. The river was a nondescript brown, its current running swiftly in the same direction as the slow moving train. She saw what silenced their high spirits, paled their faces. A shape bobbed in the current, like a shop dummy, or a sack. Body shaped, head down, arms stretched out. The hands glowed pale, standing out against the body and the river. It could have been wearing white evening gloves. The three women sat, moving alongside, their eyes fixed upon it, carried downstream buffeted slightly by the current. Raindrops rippled the water's surface into wide circles.

For Rats it was one more omen. Another indication that death lay everywhere in this city. She half expected the cry of the brakes and the jolting halt that signify a death on the tracks. Turning away, she looked down at her feet, held her hands up to her face, flexing her fingers, then let them rest on her knees.

The two women watched through the steamy window, long past the point where they could have still seen the body. They turned away from the window with some reluctance, sat back in their seats. The one with the cigarettes brought them out, taking one for herself and one for her friend. She passed it across without a word. Her friend lit them both. They sat subdued, smoking their cigarettes. The train continued through Hackney. All three women got off at the same stop. Rats saw them pause on the platform, casting around for someone. They lighted upon the guard signalling the train out of the station. Rats watched as they went up and spoke to him, saw him raise his arm to point directions to them. They stood there awkwardly, then moved towards the exit. Rats followed, saw the crowds close in and carry them away from her as effortlessly as the river had swirled the body and its white, white hands.

13

Rats came home through wet streets. Dalston was busy with late night shoppers. Stall holders shouted the odds on their trade. The last pickings of tomato, pineapples, avocadoes were being sold off cheap. Buy anything and you'd get the same again thrown in for half price. People laden with shopping trolleys were fighting their way on to buses and plastic bags threatened to burst all along the queue. Harassed women trundled supermarket carts stacked with cardboard boxes to where their husbands vied and jockeyed for a place to park between the pelican crossing and the bus stop. Children trailed in their wake, dragging economy size washing packets, toilet rolls on special offer.

She knew she should make her way in there too, to buy her weekly purchases. She couldn't face it, shopping for one in the crush of families and couples. If she went in there she'd buy at random, absentmindedly purchase too much for her needs, the pressure to be seen buying for two. She would probably come out with a bag too heavy from the weight of a bottle to carry in comfort.

There was no comfort in the crowded street for Rats as she stood outside the pie and mash shop watching the eels slowly writhe beneath the bloodied chopping board. She couldn't face going home and headed for the Railway. The back bar was empty, as it usually was early evening. Peter had a pint drawn for her as she came up to the bar.

'And how are we tonight?'

'Wet,' she smiled, 'not to mention fed up.'

'And what's a fine young woman like you got to be fed up about?' He was handsome in his way. And his banter never irritated Rats the way it might have done. She guessed because his friendliness was an easy, casual thing for the men as well as the women using his bar, the young and old alike.

'Why don't you stay for the sing-along? That'll take your mind off things. Sean and the crew'll be along any time now.'

'Maybe,' said Rats, picking up her glass.

Peter turned away to serve the customers in the other bar, Rats walked over to the seat by the Ladies toilet. She tried to avoid looking in the mirrored door. She wanted to avoid having to recognise and own up to that tense, bedraggled figure that she knew would lower out at her if she raised her eyes. As she sat and drank her beer, she fingered the wad of notes in her pocket. Maybe it was only Ralph's conscience, prompted perhaps by thoughts of what Maureen would have to say about her being sacked that had made him give her the equivalent of an extra three weeks' money. But it seemed in her heightened state almost a threat or a bribe. The problem was, she didn't know what her silence was being bought for.

The longer she sat and drank, the less likely it seemed that a firm like Lindy's would bother to cushion her sacking – there had been definite hostility. She sat, turning that over in her mind, explaining it and trying to square it with the money. Because Ralph had said 'your sort of person' to her, she found it easy to take that to herself as prejudice. She had, after all, spent many years facing it directly and indirectly. She didn't need anyone to spell it out for her. But over the years too, she had learnt to be more circumspect, wary of people and did not easily or willingly give anything away about herself. He must have worked hard to find it out, or seen her around town, or been told. Men often prided themselves on being able to spot a lesbian. What they usually meant was they had encountered a woman, often casually, often accidentally, who refused their attentions. Ralph had not seemed that kind of man. It seemed an unlikely explanation for her sacking. It made a mockery of the money.

Rats bought a second pint, the bar was filling up and Sean, a mountain of a man, began to fiddle with the amps and microphone balanced on top of the piano. Rats continued to puzzle over the meaning of 'your sort of person' as the piano tinkled and crashed into life and Sean's average but enthusiastic voice boomed out an over-amplified version of 'Danny Boy'. He'd done 'Coward of the County', 'The Town I Love the Best' and 'The Rose of Tralee' before she came back to the explanation she'd been trying to avoid. It all led back to Pershing, his car, the body. The fear seemed ridiculous, safe as she was in this pub. A terrible isolation descended upon her, drunk as she was from downing her beer fast on an empty stomach. Her maudlin spirits were in tune with the rest of the pub as Sean launched into 'A Bunch of Thyme'. She felt the tears prick and swallowed the lump in her throat as the chorus swelled around her. It was a song you'd find on every jukebox of every Irish pub in London, part of the repertoire of every singer who gets up to do a Friday night spot in these same pubs for the Irish working class drowning its sorrows in English Guinness.

The song was part of her childhood. Her party piece at family get-togethers and she couldn't hear it without seeing herself, nine years old in a well washed emerald green cotton frock, singing out of key and out of tune under the benign eyes of her mother and father, the aunties and uncles and the endless cluster of her cousins. Finishing her drink, she left, the tune running in her head. Instead of catching the bus home she walked down towards the junction into a phone box. She pushed a coin in and made contact.

'Brenda, it's me, Rats. Can you do me a favour?' Rats paused, Brenda waited. 'I've got to go away, sudden. Can you feed my cat, I'll drop the keys around.'

Brenda wanted to know where she was going, why and for how long. She also had a better idea about the keys. Rats wasn't able to be wholly honest with Brenda, she knew her decision and values wouldn't stand questioning, especially not as drunk as she was now. She made a vague explanation.

'Okay, a couple of days, not long. I'll leave them in the Railway.' Brenda asked no more questions, Rats had no more to say, she hung up.

Pushing her way through the crush at the bar she waited to catch Peter's eye. When he came over she explained the situation and handed over her keys. He put them into a plastic coin bag and left them by the till.

'Take care of yourself now.' And she was gone. Walking towards the bus for King's Cross.

The journey took the best part of forty-five minutes. The Angel was a bottleneck day and night and the bus she was on chugged and stopped and started its way through the eight-lane tangle of cars, lorries and exhaust fumes. It was only four more stops before the familiar concourse of King's Cross and her test of nerve. It was possible to simply cross the road and take a bus back. She wasn't committed to anything and as the false confidence of drinking on an empty stomach wore off so did the idea of taking off out of the city. But the wad of notes and her failure of nerve rubbed against her and returning to Hull seemed to hold out the promise of relief, if not release.

She came into the heart of the station to the sound of platform announcements, the rattle of the notice board ticking out the latest departures and crowds of people. King's Cross was never quiet; each platform had its resolute queue, snaking back across the concourse marked by trolleys and suitcases. She walked through to the booking office. There was a choice of trains. The 9.25 and the 00.07. The 9.25 would get in at a quarter to midnight, being a 125. The 00.07 would get in at 6.15, being a stopping train. She had nowhere to go when she arrived, had notified no one of her coming. The 6.15 seemed more manageable and travelling seven minutes into Saturday meant she could buy a Saver. It saved her the trouble of having to decide whether she was going to buy a return or not.

Rats had the best part of three hours to kill. She wandered back into the newsagent's, bought things to read, cans of drink and chocolate. Then she went out into the night air.

King's Cross is no place to linger. Wide boys, lushes and junkies bounded by the cruising taxi-drivers. Young girls looked to turn tricks, nervously, as if this was an activity new to them, like wearing make-up and borrowing their older sister's clothes. For a good few of them it probably was. An easy way to pick up money, aside from all else they would be picking up with it. The experienced ones worked the side streets and the hotels, out of sight unless you went looking for them in the maze of seedy council flats behind the station.

Rats side-stepped a group of drinkers going through the motions of a fight while a young policeman cast a bored eye over them. Past Bravington's brash adverts for diamonds and engagement rings and into a pub. Friday was women's night. It had a sign saying Private Function on the door and a table where you paid 75 pence. Like most gay bars, you paid to go in. A small price, 75p for knowing that the greater number of the women gathered around you were dykes, free of casual male drinkers.

It was a large L-shaped room with a reputation as a women's bar, rather than strictly lesbian. Rats bought herself a pint and some quiche and salad. She sat nearer the pool table than the disco to eat it, her back against the wall, her feet on a stool, surveying the scene. Reaching for the last of her pint, she decided to have a second. The place was filling up now, fast. Mostly groups of three or four, lots of couples. The illusion of everyone but you knowing everyone else.

Two women sat next to her. The younger one was all eyes, eagerly watching the people coming in, the women with their arms around each other's waists and shoulders, taking in the kissing and dancing as if she'd never seen it before. The older woman with her sipped her half of lager and looked like she could think of at least a dozen better ways to enjoy herself on a Friday night. The young woman was making eye contact, she was either going to have to talk to her or brazen it out. If she was smoking she could sit there steadfastly blowing mouthful after mouthful of smoke in a slow steady stream that said 'keep off', knock ash into the ashtray in a no-nonsense, occupied way. But one of the reasons she had stopped smoking was the need to confront rather than evade life.

As these thoughts went through her head, the younger woman spoke. 'Do you come here often?'

She turned to them, the older woman looked embarrassed and peered into her drink with all the concentration Rats had applied to hers less than a minute previously. The younger woman was all enthusiasm, she didn't want or need an answer. She was off, bubbling over with her own story. Rats recognised her accent; Scunthorpe. Quickly Rats realised she wasn't being picked up, the girl was just eager to talk. She must have been all of nineteen, the woman with her twenty-six or twenty-seven.

For quite a few years she had thought she might be a lesbian, not that she had known the word or what that meant. She just felt different from her other friends, bored by boys, thought them and 'it' a bit of a waste of time. Della, her sister, was the only person she'd told. It was she who found out about the clubs in London and suggested they go down for a weekend. They had just arrived, were staying at the London Brothers Hotel further up Euston Road. And how does Della know about London's gay scene wondered Rats, but Della's role appeared purely sisterly. She went to the bar, bought drinks for the three of them and seemed genuinely pleased that Janice had found someone to talk to. Janice seemed so too, running on with her monologue. 'And I just wanted to see, you know, what it was like. Not to get off with anyone, really. Just have a look round. Our Della's great. I'd never have come on my own. She's just come to give me moral support, haven't you Della?'

'Yes, love,' Della put the drinks down, seemed indifferent to the conversation and her surroundings.

Rats and Janice chatted on about clubs and bars and places to go. Rats said she was catching a train that night but fancied a dance before she went so they fought their way through to the small, crowded dance floor. They moved around, close to each other and at a suitable moment Rats put her arms around Janice, drawing her in and dancing close. As the track finished she said: 'Got to go now,' and they walked back to finish the drinks and take their leave of each other.

'Enjoy yourself now,' Rats called back leaving them to last orders and the strains of Gloria Gaynor's 'I Will Survive'.

It was a long time since Rats had been back to Hull. It had been an impulse to return, a need to be somewhere familiar, safe. Somewhere, too, the impulse came from a need to be with Helen again, to at least talk with her about what had happened. When it came down to it, Helen was the only one she trusted enough to talk with about the events of the last six months. She wasn't going back to a place but to a person.

The guard waved them through the barrier. The engines came to life and the train pulled out of the station, gathering speed as it cut through the dark, lighted windows and street lamps blurring to a smudge.

As Rats sat behind her newspaper the newsprint came in and out of focus. The train rattled out a chant, Rats was too tired to fight. They left London behind. Money and death, money and death it ran, on and on until it rocked her, finally, into a fitful, dreamless sleep, her head resting on her folded hands, leaned against the window. She might have been praying.

14

Rats was woken by the dawn. She went through to the toilet, bracing her body against the rise and fall of the train. Discounting the notice not to drink the water, she sluiced her mouth round with the warm, brackish liquid. She wanted a cup of tea or coffee, but there was no buffet car. She had the second can of beer from the night before, but to drink it would set the wrong note for the coming days. There was a little over an hour left of the journey. The train ran along the broad estuary of the Humber.

In the spare grey light of early morning the river looked cleansing, as if in the hours of darkness it had drawn into itself all the grime and grit of the land beside it to rinse it fresh and clear for the new day. As they neared the main port and city, they passed industrial workplaces: ship repairers, cranes and warehouses, small wharves. Isolated light ships gave way to a definite pattern of buoys guiding a route along the waterway. Passing through small towns and villages, the scatter of farms and manor houses on the flat land gradually gave way to bigger towns that finally merged. They were still moving at speed as they passed the flyover on the outskirts of the city, but slowed as they came to the new hospital, taller than its surrounding buildings, casting a grim clinical shadow of ill-fortune over the mean streets it stood amongst. Then the lurch of the brakes and the multilingual station name plates. Welcome to Kingston upon Hull, Bienvenue, Wilkommen. It was just after six.

The station buffet was open, but Rats needed something stronger. She joined her fellow passengers, streaming out across the concourse in search of taxis, friends and relations, disturbing the city's stillness. Buses had the roads almost to themselves. A road sweeper pushed a hand cart, there was the occasional lorry from the docks, a small stream of taxis and cars brought together by the London train.

Rats toyed with the idea of going across to the bus depot canteen. She had been friendly with one of the women who worked there, Katie. It had been a while since she had seen her, but Katie wasn't the sort of woman to let that stand in the way of a mug of tea and a bacon sandwich. But that would be a connection, need an explanation why she was there, what she was doing. Anyway, she could as easily be working the two-to-ten as the six-to-two shift. Standing outside the station entrance, Rats gradually let the familiarity of the scene take hold. She needed anonymity, time to plan her actions. After buying a newspaper, she asked where she would find a decent cafe close by. The woman paused for thought, 'All these, you know, precinct places they'll be closed now until nine o'clock. You want to go down by the market. Not the market hall mind, the proper market down by the pier.'

Rats set off for the market through the main shopping streets, beyond the town hall and municipal buildings, the empty dock, the college and Queen's Gardens, on across the Market Square and down streets that suddenly narrowed, tarmac giving way to cobbles, while on either side rose tall warehouses. The doors of one were open and men with forklift trucks and trolleys moved about inside, lorries backed up into them and the sounds of hard and fast manual work drifted out. Rats carried on until she came upon a group of three men leaning against a lorry they had just stacked with crates of fruit. Asking if there was a cafe close by, they directed her across the road, down the second on the right to Al's. 'Tell him we sent you,' they called out after her.

Al's was a no-nonsense, steamy hub of warmth and tantalising smells. The place was almost full, men of all ages in the drab serviceable clothes of heavy work. A pall of smoke rested on the steam from the urn and the roll-up tins were passed around as easily as the newspapers. They looked her over when she came in, but no more. A girl of maybe sixteen came to take her order, putting up with a fair amount of calling and back-chat but giving as good as she got. Rats ordered the breakfast, with tea.

'Cup, pint or half-pint?' asked the girl. Rats settled for a half pint, no sugar.

She took her newspaper out, unfolded it and began to read, thinking the while what to do now that she was here. She decided to get herself sorted out at the YWCA, it would be cheaper than a hotel and Rats needed to watch her money. She had brought nothing with her, she would have to buy a few essentials. As she made out a list she regretted not having planned the trip properly. But even as she did so, contemplating the array of eggs, bacon, sausage, tomatoes and mushrooms before her, she knew that properly planned she would never have come. Had she stayed drinking in the Railway all evening and then gone home to plan she knew that, sober the next morning, she would never have set out. To do a thing like that, in cold blood,

74

was to act spontaneously. And Rats rarely did things on the spur of the moment.

So why was she here? Away from London, her fear diminished but she remembered it and knew she was in Hull because of that most basic of instincts, flight. As she mopped up the juices on her plate with a piece of toast, she reached the third item on her mental list. She must ring Helen.

With this thought, Rats' stomach churned and the relish she had taken in her food evaporated. It lay, a lardy mass on her stomach as the prospect of phoning Helen did on her mind. They had parted, called themselves friends, in word alone. And since then they had had no contact with each other. But the need to phone her was urgent, as solid as her own self, sitting in the cafe's early morning bustle.

Agitated at the prospect of calling Helen, wondering what they would have to say to each other, she decided to think it over as she walked. Leaving the cafe, she cut through an alley that brought her up on to the pier front.

Once upon a time there had been a ferry plying its trade between the pier and New Holland. Now with the Humber Bridge it was obsolete, withdrawn from service. Although the journey took all of twenty-five minutes, the ferry boat had boasted a snack bar and a licensed bar. A return trip, never disembarking, had been a rare family treat. Like many men who work with ships, her dad had a fascination for them. He would delight in taking herself, Pauline her sister and Kieran her brother out for a trip on the ferry. There would be crisps and orange squash for them, a bottle of pale ale for himself and they would all, in their minds, make it a greater expedition than it was.

The ferryboat had been paddle operated. When the sight of the wake churning behind them as the boat turned into the full channel paled, they would go below decks to watch the pistons drive the paddles round. All the boat's workings were brass and wood, highly polished and well preserved, as if anticipating the day it would cease as a working concern and become a museum piece, taken out on holidays for excursion trips, moored the rest of the year as a floating exhibit.

Now Rats walked around the pier frontage, watching the waves lap against the high wall, seeing the mud and water swirl under the cracks in the wooden pier. As she breathed in the cool, clear air off the river, she registered the fish. That smell so distinctive to the city you forgot it whilst you lived there, but were overpowered when you returned. It was not unpleasant, and as her senses adjusted, she found its familiarity oddly reassuring.

The tang in the air had at first woken Rats up, but it was soon emphasising her tiredness. It was coming on nine o'clock, so she made her way back to the city centre, purchased her few requirements and set out to find herself a room. Rats took a bus out to the YWCA on Westbourne Avenue. She had lived over off the Dock Road; this area, the Avenues, was unfamiliar. They lay on one side of Spring Bank West, Rats had lived further away, on the other side of the Anlaby Road, running parallel to it. It got its name from the leafy broad avenues with fountains at the large roundabouts that had once served as turning areas for horses and carriages. Some of the houses had been converted into flats, others were owned by the University.

Rats had been over this way a few times to large sprawling student parties where nobody knew who you were and nobody cared. She and Helen had been a few times to meetings in somebody's house. Two women who did not usually use the club had been handing out leaflets at the Contessa about a plan to set up a Lesbian Line. Their leaflet made sense of Rats' and Helen's experience of isolation. They decided to go along, but the meetings were not a success for them. All the other women there were students; all Helen and herself had in common with these others was their sexuality and they, unlike the other women, were not in the habit of speaking up, or out, about it. Lacking common ground for discussion or friendship with these women, as the project drifted, so did they.

The YWCA was at the start of the Avenue, facing onto Pearson Park, a four-storey, functional building with a fire escape running down the side which backed onto an alley. Rats went in. She paid for three nights, in advance. Taking her towel and key, she went up stairs to her room. She took out her new flannel, her soap, toothbrush and paste and went in search of a bath. The bathroom was as functional as the rest of the building, but the water was hot and relaxing. As Rats dressed she felt drowsy, so decided to lie down for an hour or two.

At two Rats woke, wondering at first where she was. The sickly yellow cast of the room came into focus and she remembered. Rising from the bed, she straightened her hair, pulled down her jumper and put her shoes back on. She went down stairs and out of the building.

remembering to keep her key. She wanted the privacy of a public phone box; there was one directly opposite the building. For a brief moment Rats hoped it was out of order.

Inside the box she paused before dialling the all too familiar number, once her own. A voice she did not recognise spoke to her. There was a pause. It was a simple enough thing to do and Rats did it, conscious of her stomach tilting over and the tremor of her hands. 'Could I speak to Helen please?'

There was a pause before the voice spoke again. 'She's not here, I'm afraid.'

'She still lives there though?'

Another pause, 'Yes.'

'Will she be in later?'

'No.'

It was like a guessing game. Was she on holiday, away for the weekend, out for the day? Finally the woman at the other end asked who she was.

As if in response to direct questioning, Rats asked her own. 'Is there some reason why I can't speak to Helen?'

'Yes,' replied the woman and continued, unconvincingly, 'she isn't here.' The reticence was tangible. 'She may not want to speak to you, she's not well at present, in fact . . . ' The voice trailed off.

Rats was puzzled and worried. Was Helen critically ill? In a coma? She had staked so much on coming back to Helen. She was shocked that Helen wasn't there for her. In the space of seconds the world turned ominous.

The pips came and went in silence. Rats grasped for a way out; she thought she'd found it. 'Are you in touch with her? Could you ask her if she'll speak to me, can you do that?'

The woman responded to the urgency in her voice, 'Yes,' she said, evidently relieved. 'Yes, what a good idea. I'll ask her, what did you say your name was again? Rats, okay. Can you phone tomorrow morning, about eleven?'

Rats remembered to ask who she'd been speaking to. She wrote it down on a piece of paper: 'Debbie, 11 a.m., Sunday'. They rang off. It felt good to have it over even if Rats was now left with more questions than she'd started with.

15

There was time to kill before tomorrow morning and Rats didn't know what to do with herself. She felt her self-control slipping away. Her anxiety was at a pitch she had only ever experienced momentarily. Never before in her life had anything been as sustained as this unease. London, so far away now, seemed unreal. Walking the streets of her home town she imagined herself awake in a bad dream. Everything, from splitting up with Helen to finding the body to losing her job seemed insubstantial set against the reality of this place, this time. The fear of seeing anyone she might know suddenly overwhelmed her. The prospect of spending the evening alone terrified her. In her agitation she walked halfway through Pearson Park before she was conscious of having come into the park at all. She had to calm down, her skin itched with tiredness, her reactions were edgy. It was July and the flower beds were coming into their own, but Rats barely noticed them.

By the time she reached Beverley Road, she had decided to get herself a decent meal, walk through the town centre and see if there was anything on at the pictures. A jumble of contending thoughts played around her conscious and unconscious mind. First, the telephone call and her realisation that in coming back she had imagined Helen just as she always had been. Now the knowledge that Helen was ill made her wonder just how she fared, whether she had changed at all. She had come to Helen in crisis, to the Helen she knew. Dependable, innovative, strong. She wanted to be taken in her arms, hushed, soothed and comforted. Helen's absence pushed her back to the death and the incidents following it which she now saw as linked and sinister. Alone again with that fear, she despaired.

Rats walked through a town centre whose familiarity was shadowed behind the harsh new lines of shopping precincts and multi-storey car parks, anxious about bumping into anyone who knew her. It was unnecessary, part of her general fears. Her married sisters lived on the new estate, Bransholme. Her mother rarely shopped in town and her father would be dozing in front of the Saturday TV sport after a few pints in the pub on the corner of their street.

Rats stood on Princess Bridge and watched the wind ruffle the water of the Dock, empty now as it had been for the last forty years, when war-time bombing had demolished the channels linking it into the system. Too expensive to put back into commission, too deep to be drained and landscaped like the Queen's dock, now a riot of colour, an oasis of leafy green. Princess Dock stood there, reminding her of other tracts of water, out of sight behind high bricked dock walls, taken out of commission by an enemy more effective than any war-time bombing. Rats, remembering the vast expanses of empty dockland in London, wondered what the situation was like here, whether her father was still working.

He wasn't old enough to take early retirement or young enough to learn another trade. And her mother – were they still in the same house, where she fought a mean battle with dirt and grime, a battle of making ends meet, making do, making the best of things? Over the years, her mother's lips had become thinner and thinner, drawn into a tight line of resignation and restraint. Rats could never imagine they had ever been as plump, full and pink as her own. Now, she thought, those lips must be thin as a thread, pulled across a face watching her family, and the families all around, as they slid back from the precarious rungs of progress they appeared to have gained in the last thirty years.

Rats had an urge to take a bus out to the fish dock, just to remind herself it was still there. It would go past the end of her street and she could gaze out, hoping to catch a glimpse of a familiar figure, reassure herself that the area hadn't been cleared, her family moved out to some newer, grimmer housing development. But the afternoon was drawing on, and she was playing with the idea of her family. Much as she felt for them and their struggles in this cold and windy city, she had no routes back to them. It wasn't as easy as catching a bus.

Their anger when they'd found out about Helen cast a shadow down the years. She had sinned against the Holy Virgin Mary and all the saints and martyrs of the Catholic Church. But her greatest sin was against the family, the Holy Family and her own. And that put her forever beyond its pale. That and her unwillingness to accept that what she was, and felt, was wrong. For weeks there had been rowing, fighting and tears. The recriminations seemed endless. Rats always believed her mother would come round after a while, and then, with all her years' practice at it, make possible a peace with the rest of the family. But her mother had been the hardest on her, taken to heart what she saw as failure. A wall came down between them. Her mother had stopped speaking to her, refused to have her at the table with them, though she continued to cook her meals as she always had. And she refused to touch the rent money, letting it lie in the fruit dish on the sideboard, week after week. Rats had taken it with her when she finally left, using it towards the deposit on the flat she rented with Helen.

Her father had been more direct and she found that easier. Making no attempt to understand her, he simply decided to beat it out of her. And when he realised it wasn't to be beaten out, he cursed her to the devil and the English. Only twice before had he taken a strap to her. Once when she was eight and slammed the front door so hard it broke the glass lights. The second strapping had been a few years later when he found her and two younger cousins in his bedroom, smoking dimps out of the ashtray beside his bed. Then her mother had stood by, giving approval to the punishment, but when he had buckled up his belt and gone to the pub or the betting office, she applied cold water and soothing cream to the red weals on her backside and thighs and soothed the crying by rocking her gently across her knees to take the pressure off the sores.

That final beating had been unwitnessed and unrestrained. Coming home late, she had stumbled upon her father brooding in the kitchen. Although she turned away from his taunting abuse, he had been too fast for her, putting his bulk between them, blocking off her escape. The kitchen was too small to evade him for long, his fury too powerful for her to resist. And instead of a terse, 'You are a great disappointment to your mother and me, Geraldine, a great disappointment,' it had been a string of curses that echoed every dockland bar her father had ever got drunk in. And when, finally, he had ceased to swear and curse and flay her and gone upstairs to bed, there had been no comfort from her mother. Rats had to stay away from work until the bruising went down. She lost her job.

She was as sure he would never lay a finger again on her as she was that he no longer saw her as his daughter. But it was her mother that made her go, not for anything she said but knowing she must have lain awake upstairs. Listening first to the row, her voice rise and break with desperation, refusing to deny where she had been, who she had been with. Lain, listening to him in a drunken rage beat the living daylights out of her.

Rats would have liked to be able to walk in and make a fresh start, pick up the threads of gossip, the interweaving of change and continuity in their lives. But if anything, time would have hardened their resolve. She had ceased to exist for them. The family had simply opened to allow her to fall away, then closed over her head as completely as broken water finds its own level, moving on and over her.

Rats ate, bought some whiskey on her way back to the YWCA and felt her anxieties lessen under the pressure of tiredness. She was soon asleep and her sleep was untroubled. She woke early the next morning; her room faced east and the sun streamed in. She glanced through the Sunday papers in the lounge, declined offers to accompany fellow residents to morning services and made desultory conversation with those as disinclined as herself to honour the Sabbath.

Rats made her phone call. Debbie sounded friendlier, more relaxed than on the previous day.

'Hello, it's Rats here.'

'Hello Rats, Debbie. I spoke to Helen last night. She was surprised you'd been in touch, but she will see you. If you want to see her.'

'That's great. How do I see her?' Rats laughed a nervous little laugh, 'What's the secret code then?'

Debbie sounded as if she was frowning down the line. 'I'm sorry if it sounds ridiculous to you, Helen isn't well, I told you that. She doesn't really want to see people. And she's in hospital. She's been very ill, with hepatitis.'

Rats wasn't sure what hepatitis was, but hospital sounded serious enough. 'I'd no idea. I'm sorry. When can I see her?'

'This afternoon if you like. They're fairly flexible about visiting. She's in the General, ward eleven. If you're definitely going we won't.'

'Yes, I'll go today.'

'Well, then, we might see you up there sometime. So long.'

Rats put down the receiver and stood, recovering her composure.

16

Rats decided to take a chance on the visiting hours. Calling back at the hostel for her jacket, she set out to walk to the hospital. As she walked she thought not about herself and life in London, but about Helen. Not the Helen ill in hospital, she could barely stand to think about that, but the woman she had known and loved. Rats wondered whether she'd have changed at all.

They could never agree about when they'd first met. Rats always spent Saturday afternoons with a group of old school friends in the cafe across from the Central Library. They would drink coffee, smoke and gossip, wander around the shops together, indulging themselves by trying on clothes and shoes too expensive for their weekly wages. Over the years, the group changed. Girls married, or had babies, and dropped out, caught up by housework and family commitments. Sometimes a work-mate or a sister would be invited and gradually become one of the gang. They were a familiar sight in the cafe and got on well with the manageress and the waitresses.

Helen worked in Marks and Spencers with Sally Murgatroyd and started to come along with her on her free Saturdays. She always maintained she was aware of Rats from the start, intrigued by her quiet domination of the group, her irreverence about boys and dates. Gradually they got into the habit of arranging to meet on Saturday evenings to go to the clubs and discos. Usually they met men at these places who bought them drinks and slobbered over them on the dance floor but rarely took them home. They preferred each other's company, bored by the bravado and crudity of men looking to score, weighing up their attractions, competing for the attention of whoever appeared more favourable, angling to pair off the rejected one with their graceless friend.

After a time they chose to go to quieter pubs together or the folk club and got into the habit of spending evenings at each other's houses. They talked about their lives, their hopes and ambitions. The buses stopped running too early for all they had to say to each other and then Rats would stay over at Helen's. Unlike Rats, Helen was an only child, her mother recently divorced. Rats enjoyed being in Helen's house, it was peaceful and orderly, her mother was fond of

Rats and would often join them in the evening to talk about her life, telling them stories about her time in the Wrens, warning them against men, telling them they were too young to settle down, not to make the mistakes she had.

One night, some months after Rats had started staying over, she and Helen had gone to bed rather drunker than usual. Helen's mother was away at a friend's in York and they had bought vodka and lime to drink instead of the cider she approved of. It was a hot night and daringly drunk they slept naked in her mother's bed. Rats remembered the sensation clearly, the cool sheets on her sweating body, the floating effect of the alcohol and the acute consciousness of her breathing, irregular and fast. They lay side by side on their backs, giggling over some joke, only a sheet covering them.

They turned to each other at almost the same moment, surprised by the kiss, so unlike those they were used to enduring from men. Touching breasts and bellies, they moved against each other, gently clumsy as they found the moist centre between their legs. In the morning they didn't talk about what had happened. It took a long time to talk about it, to admit their pleasure, each risking the other's rejection.

Approaching the hospital, Rats remembered vividly the night they had been woken by a phone call in the early hours. The desperate panic to find a taxi, the slow motion journey to this same place where Mrs Murray lay critically ill after a heart attack. Then the hospital had been almost deserted, a porter had taken them up to the intensive care unit and they had stood in shocked silence in the corridor as a doctor and nursing sister explained what had happened and what they were doing. Helen had virtually run from the house, run into the hospital, now her energy left her and she sagged against Rats. They weren't allowed to see her mother immediately. The nurse brought chairs and hot, sweet tea in yellow melamine cups. Helen's hand shook too much to hold it, scalding herself as she put it down.

When they were taken in to the ward Mrs Murray was barely conscious and seemed at first not to recognise them. Rats recalled the shock of seeing her, semi-naked and vulnerable amongst the machines now keeping her alive. She looked suddenly old; her skin grey, her eyes vacant with pain and fear. Helen held her hand, kissed her forehead and tried to speak, but only tears came.

The doctor told them she was stable and the best thing they could do now was to get some sleep and come back in the morning. At home, Rats had lain awake with Helen, who clung to her, sobbing and calling for her mother, like the baby she had once been. Mrs Murray died three days later.

It was with these memories that Rats entered the hospital and received directions to ward eleven. She was early for visiting but the ward sister let her in when she explained she had come from London. Helen was in a small two-bed annexe off the main ward. She was dozing as Rats went in, her freckled face turned to the wall, her gingery curls making a small dent in the pillows piled up high under her head. There was a lump in Rats' throat as she looked at her.

Helen stirred as if aware of being watched; turning her yellowed face to Rats, she smiled at her.

'Hello, I've brought you these.' Rats put the freesias on the bed cover, Helen picked them up, smelt them and smiled again.

'My favourites.'

'Of course.' Rats smiled back, pulled a chair over and sat down. She didn't know where to begin. Helen seemed exhausted by the effort of watching her. Rats felt tears in her eyes, pushed down the reasons bringing her back to Helen and reached for her hand. 'Whatever's happened to you?'

'Hepatitis, that's the medical term for it. Or you could say disappointment, unemployment, uselessness, rejection, despair. Take your pick.' Helen's tone shocked Rats, the spirited confidence she had always envied in her had given way to bitterness, a flippant self-hatred. She seemed thinner, fragile in the stiffness of the hospital bed. 'And what about you? What brings you back to the Mecca of the north-east – hardly me, I imagine.'

'I did come back to see you but now I'm here, with all this . . .' Rats wavered, a nurse came into the room before she could continue. She was relieved to be asked to wait outside as the screens were pulled round Helen's bed.

In the corridor Rats puzzled over the changes in Helen. The illness, obviously, affected her physically but Rats wondered whether it was wholly responsible for her world weariness. It disturbed her. Helen had always had the courage and confidence Rats lacked. Their years together had stretched her, pushed her into taking risks, living dangerously and learning to enjoy it. Helen's exhilarating loving had let her abandon her cautious timidity, she had flourished with her as she had not done since. The recent events in London and the formless, depressed months before them had been threaded with her sense of the loss Helen was to her. She had come back needing Helen's help to make sense of it all and give her encouragement to continue. Instead she found Helen defenceless, in need herself.

By the time the nurse let her go back to Helen, Rats had decided to keep quiet about her own problems for the time being. She asked what the nurse had wanted and they moved from there to a general discussion about her illness and the likely length of time she would be in hospital. It was soon time to go; Rats promised to come back the next day.

Walking back, Rats felt there were things she needed to know about how Helen had been living that she couldn't ask her directly. She wondered who Debbie was – a friend, a lover perhaps. She phoned her before she went into the hostel; neither of them wanted to talk over the phone but they agreed to meet the following day. Rats made a note of the time and the place, the art gallery.

17

The night seemed never ending. Rats drank her whiskey. She sat on the side of her bed, head in hands. She sat in the lounge, chattering inconsequentially above the ripple of half-watched TV programmes. She went to bed but every time she closed her eyes, the institutional form of her own room became the ward Helen slept or lay awake in. And every time she tried to reach her she couldn't and everytime she'd try to speak to her, her mouth moved soundlessly.

Mid-morning found Rats walking across the marble floor of the art gallery to keep her appointment with Debbie. She could see the cafe, like a circle of heaven. Its tables and chairs were ranged along the outer rim of a balcony, allowing customers to look down on to the gallery and its visitors. As Rats walked underneath it, looking for a way up, she wondered if Debbie was looking down on her. She found the steps and went up them, two at a time.

She walked around the tables, inspecting the people sitting at them, looking for a woman wearing a beige cardigan. She didn't find her. She sat down at a vacant table and ordered tea for two and toasted teacakes, leaned back and waited. She knew Debbie as soon as she walked into the cafe. She was of medium height and build, her hair mid-brown, her clothing, from beige cardigan to polished brown sandals, merged into safe predictability. Rats was surprised by her and relieved. Seeing her, she knew there was no possibility she was Helen's lover. Respectability was stamped all over her. But then, as Debbie registered her presence and her eyes moved quickly from the leather jacket to the face free of make up, to the jeans and the plaid shirt, Rats checked herself for stereotyping Debbie. She smiled and Debbie came over.

It was an awkward lunch. Debbie, Rats learned, had been a lodger in the flat for nine months. She was a student. In the course of their conversation Rats learned more about Debbie than she wanted or needed to know. She was the sort of person you absorbed, bit by bit, just by being near her. Rats also learnt about Helen, and some of what had brought her to the situation she was in.

It was by no means an unusual story or an uncommon one. Debbie was coy, to cover her embarrassment, about Helen's sexuality. She seemed ignorant of Rats' past relation with Helen. She referred to a friend who had ceased to be around. Helen had taken it badly. Then Helen's firm had closed down and she had lost her job. She had tried for various things, but with no luck. Gradually a lethargy settled over her, she didn't seem to be eating regularly, had trouble sleeping, was permanently tired. Debbie described this behaviour in a non-committal sort of way, as if Rats would know exactly what she meant. 'I took no notice really, I mean people are like that. Round here especially, everybody's pretty low and if you lose your job, well, there's every reason to be. I didn't see anything unusual about it.'

Debbie paused to drink her tea. 'I can see now, though, I should have realised things were getting worse. But well, it's a dreadful thing to say but I stopped bothering about Helen. She was dragging me down, she wasn't easy to help either. I had my college work and my friends, my own life really. I'm only a lodger after all, I'm not involved with Helen. We were friendly enough, but not friends. But that aside, I could only do so much.'

It was said in a rush, a confession Rats supposed. It wasn't her place to judge Debbie, it wouldn't have occurred to her to do so. These things happen. Rats was in no position to judge.

Debbie took her silence, and her small, quick smile for

understanding. She went on, 'Helen wouldn't go out. She didn't seem to have many friends, and the ones she did have seemed to stop coming. She'd pick fights, arguments about nothing with them sometimes. It was the only time she stirred herself, if she was really angry. Most of the time she just stopped in bed, for days on end. And then she'd be up in the night. It was hard to live with – for me, I mean. It must have been hard for her too, but I didn't think of that. It just went on like that for weeks.'

Rats asked her how Helen had ended up in hospital.

It had all happened in the last few days. Debbie had been worried about Helen, more so than usual. She wasn't eating, felt sick and was in constant pain, every bit of her aching with terrible gripping pains in the stomach. On Friday, she had come home from college to pick up something she'd forgotten before going off with her boyfriend to spend the night at his flat.

She put her head round Helen's door to check how she was and found her being violently sick, too weak to move from the bed. The uncontrollable spasms and Helen's terrible colour made Debbie panic. She ran out to bring in Rob and together they had got Helen into a sitting position and prevented her from choking. She was not lucid, sweat poured from her and she retched convulsively long after there was anything left in her stomach to bring up. Debbie called an ambulance which had taken Helen to hospital where hepatitis had been diagnosed. Because of the delay in getting treatment she was badly jaundiced and her red blood count dangerously low.

Debbie was shaken by what had happened although Helen was out of danger now, but still weak. She would be in hospital until her blood was normal again and the infection subsiding. Then she would need a long convalescence. 'She needs to make some changes though. In a way she brought it on herself, she doesn't look after herself properly. She needs to talk about all that with somebody, I'm not the person to do it really. And she's lost touch with most of her friends.'

As she spoke, Debbie seemed to imply that Rats was the one to do this. Thinking about it Rats realised with a shock that it was rare, in all her years of knowing her, that Helen needed her. She hoped she would have the strength to pull her through.

Rats hadn't said much, beyond introducing herself as an old friend of Helen's. She asked Debbie if she wanted more tea, caught the waitress's eye and ordered it.

'If she's going to be out of hospital in a few days I could stay until then, be around when she first comes out. I'll try and talk to her, but it's difficult because of not seeing her for so long. She was so different when I knew her, I don't know where to begin.'

Debbie poured out fresh teas for them both. 'Just start there, then. Ask her what went wrong. Old friends can say these things, it's easier, isn't it? She'll listen to you.'

Rats smiled, 'Yeah, maybe it is,' thinking to herself that nothing could be harder. They finished their tea, talking generally about themselves.

Before going in to see Helen, Rats called by the nursing station.

'Are you a relation?' Nurse O'Malley asked.

'No, I'm her next of kin though, she has no relations.'

'Oh, your name isn't down here.'

'Well, I guess she was in a bad way when she came in – shall I give it to you?'

Rats learned that Helen was making good progress and would probably be discharged in a day or two. Helen was subdued; having begun to recover from the crisis that hospitalised her, she now found being there an irritant, complained of boredom. She wanted to know why Rats had come back to Hull.

Rats told her briefly, saying only that there had been trouble at work, she felt low and wanted to get away for a while.

'And couldn't you think of anywhere more exciting? You must have been desperate to see this place as an alternative. I'd rather be anywhere else.'

'Are you serious?'

'Well I don't know. It's finished up here, maybe it's no different elsewhere. You came back, didn't you?'

'I wouldn't worry yourself about it now, just concentrate on getting well. There'll be time later.'

'Oh yeah, plenty and plenty of time. It's the one thing I'm not short of.'

'You never used to have enough of it. All those meetings and campaigns and leafletting.'

'And meetings, meetings, meetings.'

They both laughed, something of the old Helen showed in her ability to laugh at herself. And laughing now made them forget the bone of contention Helen's meetings had been between them. Rats' attitude to life had been to keep her head down; she had no faith in her own or other people's power to change their lives. She was aware of injustice and admired those who took a stand against it, but her general attitude was one of resentful submission. Helen, on the other hand, could never resist a challenge. She used to joke that her greatest challenge had been persuading Rats to accept the relationship between them and with that under her belt, anything else would be easy.

It was a joke she used to cheer herself up with when times were hard, which they often were. Much of Helen's working life had been spent in shops and she had lost many a job through her union activities. Throughout the mid-seventies, Helen had been drawn into campaigns for housing action areas, against road development schemes, for abortion rights, against British troops in Ireland. Rats had privately supported her, but rarely joined her in public.

The laughter ended, Helen's bitterness returned. 'Now I've the time, I've lost the interest. All those campaigns, they came to nothing. And trade unionism isn't exactly the best hobby for the unemployed.'

'It'll come back, won't it. You're run down, give yourself a break.'

There were tears in Helen's eyes, she tried to speak but the words wouldn't come. Rats took her hand uncertainly. Helen gripped it, brought it up to her face and wiped away the tears. 'I feel such a failure. Nothing I've done amounts to anything, it's just so much wreckage. What have I ever done to be proud of?'

'Helen, you've done lots of things. Just being yourself is something to be proud of. The work you've done, the campaigns. Most of them ended because you'd won, that's not failure. And the people you've known, everything you've done for them. You're just tired, over-emotional, illness affects you like that. Come on, love, don't cry.'

As Rats spoke, she felt a gap between what she said to Helen and what she felt about herself. Helen's outpouring matched her own sense of inadequacy, her despair about her own life. But the difference was, she believed everything she said about Helen's goodness, her achievements. Where Rats' life wasn't empty, it was full of things she would rather not think about – the lost job, the dead body, her life in London. They sat a while in silence, broken by the occasional sniffle from Helen. It was almost the end of visiting time.

'I'm going to stay on a few days, I'd like to see you out before I go back to London.'

'That'd be nice. I do appreciate you being here, even if it's a funny way of showing it.'

Rats smiled, kissed her hand before she put it down, and left.

Visiting took up a small part of her day, the rest of the time Rats spent wandering around the city, walking in the parks, reading and thinking. She found herself day-dreaming about staying on, moving back in with Helen. It comforted her but she had to keep reminding herself it was a fantasy. Here, as the sleepy, summery days slowed everyone down, it was hard to imagine a world of squalor and violence, the world Rats had left and had to return to. She phoned Brenda to explain she was staying on. It was easy to let her think she had come north because of Helen's illness; Rats almost believed it herself.

On her next visit, Rats was disturbed to find Helen's bed empty. For a moment, in panic, she thought Helen was dead and nobody had told her. As she stood nervously in the doorway, a nurse came up to her. 'Oh, your sister's on the main ward now. She's doing a lot better.'

'My sister?'

'Yes, Helen Murray, isn't she your sister?'

As Rats spoke, she realised she shouldn't have. 'Oh no, she's not my sister. We're friends.'

'Oh,' the nurse looked surprised, 'well, she's down the far end, by the window.'

Rats found Helen in better spirits, she was enjoying the bustle and company of the main ward and she was confident of being discharged in the next day or two. Instead of the usual polite thank-you for Rats' gifts, she seemed genuinely pleased by today's fruit, magazines and the new P.D. James Rats had brought her. Her hair had been washed and she wore her own nightshirt instead of the hospital issue gown she had before.

'It's good to see you looking brighter. Do you feel as well as you look?'

'I feel better. I mean, I'm still glad I'm lying down with people to wait on me, but I feel as if I'm on the mend. I'm sorry about yesterday, pouring my heart out, but that was how I felt and I couldn't say it to anyone else.'

As she spoke, Helen had taken Rats' hand and was stroking it. She ruffled Rats' hair when she let it go, 'It's a good job you were here.'

'I'm glad I was. It was a shock, you think of people being how they were when you last saw them. I'd never thought of you being ill or needing things with no one to look after you.'

The ward was busy, most patients had two or three visitors. Rats and Helen stood out from the rest with the intensity of their conversation, the absent-minded ease with which they touched. Rats caught the look on the face of the woman in the bed next to Helen and tactfully withdrew her hand.

'What did you do that for? Let me hold your hand, I want to touch you.'

'Everyone's looking at us, don't.'

Helen, with no hand to hold, was stroking Rats' hair, 'So what? They're not anyway, they're too busy with their visitors.'

'That nurse isn't.'

They looked back up the ward where an auxiliary, bringing in vases for flowers, was standing gawping at them, her face rigid with disapproval.

Helen sighed and took her hands away. 'They all think you're my sister. It's amazing isn't it – you couldn't look more different from me if you tried. Dear sister, I'm glad you're here, I really am. Though I'm still puzzled as to why you're here. Was it really that bad in London?'

Rats with the confidence of Helen's improvement and her tender affection, told her the real reasons she was back. As Helen listened her face lost its contented look. 'It sounds unbelievable, completely unbelievable. You're telling the truth? You've not made it up or imagined it?'

It had taken Rats a lot to tell her, she had not expected this reaction. She felt panic return, could not trust herself to speak.

'I mean, I do believe you. It's just it sounds so incredible, that's all.' Helen abandoned their earlier caution and reached out for Rats with both her arms. 'Oh my poor love, my poor, poor love. What a time you've been having.'

In the face of such warmth Rats broke down and was comforted, long past the leaving bell, until the sister brusquely informed her she must leave and that upsetting her patients was not encouraged.

Two days later Helen was discharged. She was still weak and it would be a while before she fully recovered, but the improvement was amazing, considering how ill she'd been a week ago. Rats helped Debbie to clean up the flat ready for her return and went with her and Rob to bring her home. Debbie had cooked for them all and it was a strange, but not unfriendly, gathering. Helen went to bed as soon as it was finished, bemoaning the fact that she wouldn't be able to drink for months as she left them finishing off the beer fetched in from the Polar Bear. Rats didn't stay long; she went into Helen before she left. The sight of Helen, dozing in the bed she had shared so often with her, tucked up under a duvet cover they had chosen together, filled her with sadness.

The next day Rats was going back to London. As she packed her things she thought back over the trip. Her initial shock over Helen had worn off. She was confident Helen would come through. Helen had been lucky, though, with a chancy unpredictable luck. Rats' own fears seemed to hold less power over her now. Partly, she guessed, pouring the last of the whiskey into her tooth mug, it was the way real life people and their problems take over, pushing out the shadowy, half-imagined nightmares. Would she, as Helen urged her to do, go back and forget about it, make a new start? She wanted to, but that night, like most nights when her mind slipped slowly into sleep there was a vague unease, things glimpsed and when she first woke she carried an after-image behind her eyes. A body slumped against a car seat.

Rats went over to see Helen before she caught the train back. In hospital, the strangeness of that situation had seemed to license other departures from the norm. Rats' presence there, the tenderness between them had been unremarked upon. Now, as everyday life moved back, there was an awkwardness between them. They didn't know how to break off, how to continue contact. Helen said she had a lot of thinking to do, about herself, but also about Rats. Rats promised to write.

18

Back in London, the round of looking for jobs began. Having signed on, Rats found herself embroiled in the bureaucracies of housing benefit, just like the tenants she had unsuccessfully tried to take a stand for. Work was becoming urgent. She went each day to the Job Centre. It was tucked away in a side turning off the main shopping street, as if acknowledging its modest contribution to employment prospects. The Town Hall had a huge banner slung across it with the tally written up – 18,965 people in Hackney are out of work. One in five it said. She would wonder sometimes as she passed what her number was.

The local newspaper came out twice a week and she waited for the first copies straight from the press, along with everyone else trying to be the first in line for rented houses, flats or jobs. The ease with which Rats had got the job with Lindy's astonished her as the weeks rolled by, leaving her depressed, anxious and jobless. She was putting such energy into job-hunting she had no time for other pursuits and recreations. There was no clocking on and off, no weekends or holidays. Rats applied for jobs she had no interest in, ones she could do with her eyes shut and her hands tied behind her back.

The energy she used up looking for work took her mind off the events connected with the death, but resentment at losing her job built up. Her fear turned to anger. It was as if her curiosity, so uncalled for in the work she had to, had signalled something to Pershing. Without him knowing exactly what she knew, and without her knowing what he had done, the fact of the death and his part in it had been acknowledged between them. The sensation of being caught up in things out of her immediate control and comprehension terrified Rats. She saw no glamour or challenge in it, only a relief that she was out of Lindy's, despite her anger and depression about being unemployed. When she admitted it at all, it was as a dull leaden weight in the pit of her stomach, a cold hand on the back of her neck.

She tried to convey something of this in her letters to Helen. They wrote regularly, two or three times a week. Helen was on her way to a full recovery. The illness was a watershed for her, the culmination of a long period of self-neglect, depression and stagnation. Her letters spoke of the need for a change, nothing definite to orientate herself towards but an increasing clarity about the limits of the world she lived in.

Perhaps because they had once seen their futures in terms of each other, they refrained in their letters now from any but the most general references to anything beyond their daily lives. That they were linked to each other was undeniable, what they would do with that link was still an open question. Helen wrote to Rats asking her to visit. Rats agreed to go.

The second journey north lacked the tension of the first. She went by coach, joining the queues at Victoria threading their way between the diesel fumes and dirty coaches. She shared a seat with a middle-aged woman returning from her annual trip to see her daughter. The daughter was married to a man she had met at college. She lived in north London and never made the trip back, paying instead for her mother's annual visit. Rats' journey passed to a background lament, with no comfort to give this woman torn between personal hurt and pride at her daughter's bettering of herself.

Rats found it strange being a guest in the flat that had once been her home. Her eyes would follow the familiarity of habit and memory and find it suddenly disturbed. New cushions on the settee, different mugs hanging on the hooks she had carefully screwed into the bottom of the kitchen shelves. Debbie was staying at Rob's for the weekend so she was to have her room. It had been hers in the old days, but that was lost in the clear, uncluttered aspect it had now. The music stand and cases, the desk with neat piles of books and papers, pressed flower pictures on the walls. Rats moved the blue teddy bear pyjama case from the pillow to the armchair and unpacked her small case.

Although Helen had met Rats from the coach and taken her straight back to the flat, they found it awkward being there. They couldn't at that stage talk freely across the modest wreckage of their life together. They spent the afternoon walking along the Hessle foreshore, a scrappy stretch of sand and dunes running behind the backs of terraced houses and their neglected gardens. Their talk was general, hovering around, but never resting on the subject preoccupying them both. The question of what they were to do with each other, how they would pick up again the threads binding them to each other.

The afternoon was drifting into evening, the light taking on the blue pink that leads it to sunset.

'Do you want to go out tonight?'

'No, let's get a takeaway and a few cans, for me anyway. Have a night in.' It was the closest Rats got to saying they should talk. A pub or club would provide too many opportunities to skirt around the reasons Helen had asked her to come up for, and why she had come. Having agreed to a night in, they walked back slowly and quietly. They commented, for the sake of something to say to each other, on the gardens, cats and shops they passed. Back inside, Rats made coffee while Helen sat down to rest and they discussed what sort of food to eat.

They half watched a film on TV as they feasted on sag prawn, chicken korma, nans and bhajees. It seemed the longer the silence lasted, self-conscious about what they might hear or say, the harder it got to speak. Rats had a sudden memory, so vivid she felt a physical reaction. Herself, sitting in the cafe on the pier head on a Saturday afternoon after a swim. With Helen. She remembered the awkwardness, the clumsy sense of her body. The way she had left abruptly, almost rudely, pushing herself out of reach of the desires Helen sparked off in her. It had been Helen who had taken the initiative on that occasion, followed her out of the door, restrained her with a hand and brought her back to sit down in front of her saying, 'Don't just walk away from it, Gerry. You're taking it with you. It's not going to go away.'

She had come back at her, on edge with herself, 'What you talking about? What you going on about now?'

And Helen had said, so simply and at such cost, 'You. You and me, what we are to each other. More than friends.'

Remembering how Helen had steadily talked her through the fears and defences on that occasion, Rats felt moved to start this conversation. 'Helen, coming back here like this, it's okay isn't it?'

'Yeah, I appreciate it. It's good having you around.'

It stayed there for a while, the silence less ominous than it had been. 'Do you think we'll go on seeing each other now?'

'Depends, it's pretty expensive travelling. It's a long way. I don't know really. I think I'd like us to.'

'I find it hard though, thinking of you as a friend. It's not like it was before, not as if I can forget all that and just be friends.'

'It couldn't be. It isn't for me either. I feel differently about things now. I almost wish I'd come to London with you now.'

'Things weren't that bright between us before I went, remember. That's why I went.'

The atmosphere in the room changed subtly. Rats was conscious of touching anger in Helen. 'Maybe, but you were going anyway. For yourself, Rats, not because of me. It wasn't like that if you're honest with yourself. You were moving too fast, changing. You pushed me out, or maybe you were so damned concerned with yourself you gambled on me. And lost. We both lost.'

Rats sat for a while, thinking it over. It was hard to reach back precisely to that time. It seemed to her that Helen had been the one moving, changing. It had all been over between them before she went, she was sure of that. But somehow, where they were now made that all seem irrelevant. They were different now, their lives had changed and changed them.

'I don't want to keep going over the past. I don't see the point.'

'The point is because it forms us, it's the route that brought us here. We can't shelve it.'

Rats got to her feet, began clearing the room up, tidying the foil containers, the plates. Helen yawned, sat back on her heels, emptied Rats' can of beer into her glass.

Rats took the plates through to the kitchen, came back and sat down, close to Helen. 'There's one thing about the past I can't shelve,' she said, reaching her hand out to cover Helen's.

'More than one I'd say,' Helen's fingers curled round hers, tentatively they put their arms round each other and gently, they kissed.

'We should go to bed,' Helen said. 'It's always easier to talk lying down.'

Rats smiled a smile for all the silences they'd hoarded between the pillows and the sheets. 'Okay,' she said, standing up and giving Helen a hand to her feet.

This time, though, it was easier to talk in bed. And by morning they were getting around to a decision that involved Helen coming to London. It was partly being able to acknowledge their need for each other, partly a desire to hold fast to some stability against a frightening world. It was probably not the best basis for living together but they knew people who had done it for less.

Rats went back to London with a new resolve to find work, conscious of the need to work for herself and Helen, their new life together. Helen was to come down when she could. Debbie seemed pleased to have the place to herself, she imagined Rob would move in with her. Helen's doctor was not pleased. It did not signify recovery and the resumption of normal, everyday life to him. Helen didn't even bother to point out that the nub of her illness had lain in that normal, everyday life. Instead, she reminded herself that these men had no control over her life and contented herself with planning her departure.

She left in early September, as the city was filling up with the year's new intake of fresh-faced undergraduates. The city let her go without a murmur; London swallowed her in silence. She emerged into Stoke Newington from the number 76 bus, an eagerness in her walk, anticipation written all over her face.

19

At first energy and excitement kept them both going. They were determined to find jobs. The rediscovery and re-establishment of their relationship sustained them. Their delight in the new intimacy filled them with patience, tolerance and a sense of the appropriateness of the small flat. They had always to be within sight or sound of each other, bumped into each other moving about the place. For the time being it was another dimension to their sharing; soon, though, they knew it would begin to grate on them, become a pressure. There would be little opportunity for them to be on their own. Because the flat had been Rats' there was the danger that she would feel crowded out, Helen would feel encamped, temporary. They each wanted to deal with the problem before it started to shape them, before it actually became a problem. But before they could find another flat, they had to find jobs.

As two single women they fell through all the nets of housing provision. The council would not allow them to jointly put down their names on the list, the housing associations only accepted nominations from the council list. There was no legal obligation to house them as individuals, no recognition of their identity as a couple. Mortgages screamed out at them from the windows of the Building Societies in the High Street, estate agents mushroomed along the streets running alongside it. Flats and houses, leasehold and freehold, in need of repair and renovation, with period character, close to all amenities were everywhere around them. There was nothing under £30,000. There was no possibility of owning their own house; they were not cut out to be property owners.

At first they thought a co-op might be a possibility, then realised they were all short-life properties, in need of care and running repairs that would then be given over for rehabilitation. They found themselves resigned to the diminishing private sector.

'What about putting our names down anyway, for a hard-to-let flat?' They were sitting over coffee, the evening before them.

Rats thought for a while before she replied. 'You've not lived here long enough. I think you have to have lived here a year.'

'You could then, maybe I could say I'd lived here as well.'

'Okay, let's do that next week. Something to look forward to.'

Helen stood up and walked over to Rats' chair, she crouched by it, took her hand, 'Don't let it get you down. It's not too bad here. London's a good place to be. Let's enjoy it.'

Rats smiled at her, ruffled her hair. 'Okay, let's do that.'

Helen got up, stretched. Feeling the pressure of the confined space on her exuberance she suggested going out for a walk, maybe a drink by the river.

They walked down towards Springfield Park, the River Lea and a small pub that sold good beer. When they reached it, the evening was turning dusky. There were crowds of people standing and sitting all along the riverside. Dogs roamed about, in search of affection and crisps. From time to time they stopped and sniffed each other, sniffed the legs of the people sprawled across the small rectangle of grass. Rats and Helen took their drinks down to the furthest edge of the crowds. Against the rock and swell of the noise, they sat quietly, exchanging few words.

Children from the flats behind the pub played complicated games of tag and dare, watched with envy by the few children brought out with their parents who were obliged to sit quietly, sipping their lemonade and eating their crisps. The children from the flats, showing off their freedom made little forays towards them, calling over the dogs to pat and feed, contriving to run close up to them in their chasing games, keeping a watchful eye. The parents, absorbed in themselves and their drinks, were oblivious to the complex ritual being enacted by their offspring.

'Watch where you're going, you little bleeders,' a burly man held his drink high over the heads of a retreating foursome. 'Bleeding kids.' He passed along the walkway. The children regrouped against the wall. The three eldest girls convulsed in giggles, the younger brother puzzled over the merriment. The children with their parents became absorbed with their glasses, turned their heads down towards their feet idly kicking against the chairs. Envy had turned to relief.

As the sky grew darker, more and more people came down to the river side. The noise grew from a murmur to a steady hum, punctuated by shouted greetings, laughter that became raucous. The children melted away. The river, lapping against the sides of the bank lost its murky industrial look and became beautiful, reflecting back lights in the soft shimmer of trees further downstream. Across the marshes, trains ran at regular intervals, their lighted carriages winking with the curve and speed of the train. Occasionally overhead lines crackled and spat sparks, like lightning in the sky.

Rats and Helen sat drinking and watching the scenes around them, talking over their weeks, comparing applications they'd made, jobs that had seemed promising. 'There's nothing to keep us here, no ties.'

'I've got friends here, a few. It's familiar and where it isn't familiar, it's neutral. I find it easy being here, for all the problems.'

'We could at least look at places elsewhere. I find it overwhelming sometimes. It's exciting now, and frustrating not having the money to take advantage of everything, but sometimes I just panic. Just walking the streets, being among people, like here, who I don't know, who don't know me. I'd like to be somewhere else, somewhere slower and smaller.'

'I don't know Helen, where? Where could we go?'

'Anywhere, we're free women. We could travel, work our way through Europe, go north, south, east or west, young woman.' Helen's arms marked the compass points.

'You're mad, you fool.' Rats pulled down one of the arms, drew Helen close and kissed her. Two passing men stopped to look and jeer. One of them gestured an insult. Rats told him to fuck off but he and his friend stood their ground, leering. Rats and Helen were suddenly conscious of the dark, their distance from the crowds. The men walked on, laughing. 'Fucking queers' came back to them, a disembodied voice in the darkness. It wasn't just the chill off the river that made them shiver.

'Do you want another drink, Rats? Maybe there's a seat inside.'

They walked back to the pub, Rats went to the bar while Helen ducked between the darts players to go to the toilet. In the last hour before closing time they relaxed with the drink and the atmosphere. Helen risked asking Rats about the death. Since Hull they had barely mentioned it. Helen hoped it had receded, knowing as she wished it that something so powerful was just being silenced, kept down. Deep inside she knew this, knew the mutterings through the night and the occasional piercing scream that woke her, but not Rats, were evidence of the continuing presence in her life of that death.

'I want to know I suppose. Sometimes I do think I was mad. Am mad. But it was real. How can it just disappear like that? It was there, I saw it.'

'I know. Don't you think, though, that you have to leave it. You can't solve it. It was just something you stumbled upon. It seems to me

London's like that. All sorts of things you could stumble upon, nasty little incidents you could get caught up with. Become the victim of.'

They sat close together, concentrating. The pub mellowed around them as Helen continued talking. 'Sometimes I lie awake, the clock's green face flashing out two-thirty, three-thirty and I wonder about getting up and making a drink. And you're snuffling away beside me and the cat looks up from his nest between us. And I wonder whether it'll disturb you. And I lie there and sleep doesn't come. Deciding to get up, I slide out of bed and realise what's woken me, it's screaming or shouting. Car doors slamming, the sound of feet running. And I peer out of the window and there are a few shadowy forms in the street, or a crowd arguing on the corner spilling out onto the road. Any manner of tragedies are lived out night after night. And I let the net curtain fall and see you sleeping and the kettle clicks off. So I make my tea and take it back to bed. And it all goes on, out on the street, well into the night.'

'And I just happened to be there that time. I think that makes me feel worse, not better about it.'

'I didn't say it to make you feel bad. I'm trying to say, without undermining what you saw, or what you feel about it, that it's common. This violence is common. Maybe you should try and work out what you need to know, and why. Whether you can let it go.'

'I don't know how to do that. I don't know what I think about it. Nothing's changed since Hull. There was a death, there was a car, there was my job being connected, at least the car was owned by my boss. Other than that, I don't know.'

It was almost time to go, the bar staff were calling time and hustling people to finish their drinks. Helen took a last mouthful of her orange juice. 'This thing about the job. Why don't you go back and see them? There was no real quarrel between you and Ralph. Go back and see him, ask him.'

'Ask him what?'

'Ask him why you lost your job. Get that clear and maybe the rest will seem less powerful.'

'When you say that, I think you believe there was no connection.'

'I'm not saying there wasn't, I'm saying go and see. What you imagine is always worse than what you know.'

The sounds of the pub's closing accompanied them finishing their drinks and Rats' decision to go back and talk with Ralph. When they got back, the cat didn't run to greet them as he usually did. They stood on the doorstep, fumbling with keys, kissing each other, calling the cat quietly. Helen opened the door, Rats went back for one last look.

'Last call for the black cats,' she called out in a high pitched, squeaky voice she kept for talking to her cat. Helen was holding the door open, giggling at her.

'Get in here, you,' she said, and Rats ran back to her. The door closed behind them as they went upstairs, arms round each other.

20

Pershing ushered her into the office, indicating a seat with his arm. With that movement his elegant cuffs rode up his forearm to reveal an expensive gold watch. The office was south facing, decorated in tones that brought up the warmth and sunshine of its aspect. It was civilised and comfortable, contained solid wood furniture, discreet filing cabinets, a glass-fronted bookcase. There were pictures on the wall and the view was of the top branches of the trees.

'Have a seat,' he said, letting the 'Miss Flannagan' hang back long enough to appear forgetful, almost rude. He seated himself behind the desk. She sat where he had indicated. There was no other chair, only a small sofa under the window. The chair was low and awkward, disadvantaging the sitter. It elevated the desk and the chair behind it still higher. Cruze Pershing gave the impression of leaning forward, to look down as he spoke.

'Comfortable, Miss Flannagan?'

Something in her chest was swallowing her voice, the same something that fluttered in and out of her ribs, tickling the back of her throat. The tips of his fingers held lightly together formed an arch over the tooled leather blotter. He looked thoughtful, keeping his eyes on her as he watched her gaze move from his hands to the wall behind him, to the floor in front of her. She would not meet his eyes. He allowed the silence to rest between them. Picking up a glass paperweight, he began to speak, letting it drop from one palm to another, left to right to left.

The soft, rhythmic smack of the weight set the cadence for his slow, reasonable speech. 'Interesting, isn't it, how true these proverbs often are, even when they seem to be contradictory. Too many cooks, many hands, a stitch in time. I wonder, did these situations give rise to proverbs straight away? The first stitch in time, or whether it was the endless repetitions that beat their way into the language. How many cats, do you suppose, were killed before curiosity was seen to be the villain? Do you have a cat, Miss Flannagan?'

All his talk seemed to end in questions, but he seemed to want no answers and she had none to give him.

'I did, I've lost it.'

'Pity, were you fond of it? Women often are of their pets, especially women living alone. Probably had an accident. It's easily done. Cats don't realise their limitations. Take, for example, cats living in these flats, second, third, even higher.' Through the window, following the line of his hand, lay a high-rise housing estate.

'These cats sit looking out of windows, they see shapes and movements. All the time, dab, dab with their paws. Then someone, one day, leaves the window undone and poor puss is just a memory. Cats do dabble in things not their business. Sly creatures, wouldn't you say, Miss Flannagan?'

Rats sat there watching the smile, the stare, insolent in its confidence, watching the paperweight pass from hand to hand. Pershing had been in the office when she went back to tackle Ralph about why she was given the sack. Gone to lay the ghosts of her anxieties, prompted by Helen. She had asked her question as Ralph stood awkwardly suppressing his characteristic bonhomie. Pershing had smiled a long, slow smile at her question to Ralph. There was no trace of it left when he said, 'Come and discuss that with me, Miss Flannagan.' He had moved across the office's small space, taken a card from his wallet, pencilled a date and a time on it and handed it to her. Then he had opened the door on to the street for her, a parody of politeness.

And now she sat, ill at ease, in his expensive room, while he talked of cats and curiosity.

'You didn't ask me here to talk about cats.' She tried to look him in the eye as she said this, but the angle of the chair defeated her.

He leaned forward. 'Very perceptive, Miss Flannagan. And what do you suppose I've asked you here to talk about?'

'My job.'

'You don't have a job, do you? Now why do you think that might be?'

'I think you had me sacked. I want to know why. I want my job back.'

'I think not. We can do without you. You didn't – how can I put it – quite fit in. Why don't you just leave it, eh? There are other jobs, I believe.'

There was really nothing more to say. Rats was no wiser now than before the interview. It was as if he was playing with her. Demonstrating with his polished desk, tasteful office and solicitous secretary, that he had powers immeasurable over her. That he had no need even to speak to her, unless he chose to.

'I'll need a reference for another job.'

'But of course, how thoughtless of me.' He picked up the intercom and spoke into it. The door opened and his secretary came in. She was a young woman, well dressed, made up, her smile as permanent as the curls in her hair. She waited expectantly, with no trace of boredom or resentment in her bearing. 'Sarah, Miss Flannagan here requires a testimonial. She worked with us for four and a half months. During that time she proved to be an admirable employee. We were very sorry to have to lose her due to internal staff deployment.'

He turned to Rats, 'If you care to wait, Sarah can let you have the reference as you leave.'

He stood up, Rats hauled herself to her feet. He put an arm around her shoulder and walked her to the door. At the door he opened it to allow Sarah to go through and then proffered his right hand to Rats. She took it, feeling the soft flesh of his fingers grip harder into her own than was necessary.

As the door closed behind her, Rats saw that Sarah was already poised over the typewriter so she stood and watched while the letter was typed, taken in for a signature and then put in an envelope. She left, with some bitterness and a statement of her honesty, integrity and punctuality in her back pocket. Leaving the office, she knocked accidentally against two men coming in. She apologised; one of the men carried on regardless, the other insinuated himself closer to her, rubbing his hips against hers. 'Anytime you fancy, sweetheart.'

He lisped his words, leering at her with a badly scarred face.

She was meeting Helen in the cafe in Clissold Park. It had been Helen's idea to go back to Lindy's, to lay the ghost of Rats' fretting about the lost job. Helen was sure that the whole incident had been fomented by her imagination into something more sinister than it really was. To Helen it was a set of unconnected, arbitrary events. She refused Rats' logic. 'You'll have to go back,' she had said, 'go back and find out. It's probably very simple. He didn't like your attitude, or he thought you were stealing from him, or maybe he did know you were a lesbian and thought it would corrupt the unborn child. But for god's sake, go back and ask them.'

So, when, two days ago she had turned up at the flat with the discreet printed card, Helen had looked thoughtful but no more. 'Well,' she'd said, 'it figures, if he's the boss it probably was his decision. You must have been right about Ralph and his guilty conscience, slipping you that money.' And she left it at that, had joked with her, offering her fifty pence for every Rolls Royce she could spot in Hackney. A fiver for every corpse.

As they sat on the cafe terrace drinking tea out of thick white china cups, looking down on the children feeding the ducks, their conversation drifted. Rats kept bringing it back to Pershing, his attitude, his threats. Helen took up these threads and teased them through. She couldn't see the menace in the man. He was just a rich, bored fellow, playing his games. And to her they were just games. 'You're probably giving him a real thrill you know,' she said, stubbing out her cigarette and drinking her tea, 'you've given him star billing. Mr All Important, moving the pieces over the chess board. You and he probably watch the same cheap movies. Are you sure there weren't a couple of heavies hanging about, did you feel the bulge of the gun under his armpit as he showed you the door? And can you tell me what make it was?'

Helen was enjoying herself. Rats sat quietly, a lump in her throat and then the tears, from nowhere, were everywhere. She buried her face in her arms, stretched across the wobbly table, under the faded umbrella. Helen stopped her talk. She ran a hand through the mass of brown hair in front of her. 'Sorry,' she said, 'come on, I'm sorry.'

And as they sat like that, the tentative blue of the autumn sky turned grey and clouds scudding across were driven by a quick wind that beat the sudden downpour into their faces. They went into the cafe, ordering more tea, as the afternoon broke up and people rushed for shelter. Helen was quiet, letting Rats get over her tears. She hadn't meant to upset her, but she could be such hard work. Neither her obsession with the death nor her conviction of Pershing's part in it diminished as time passed. They left the park and went home to eat and get ready for a night out at a new women's bar with Brenda.

Helen had been reluctant to go out, she was still easily tired and couldn't drink. Mostly not drinking was all right, but she found it hard to resist the temptation in pubs and it was sometimes awkward. Being sober, she saw sides of people which were often uncomfortable. She could not so easily forget it in the morning and put it down to too much to drink. Tonight, though, she was glad to go out. It had been Rats' suggestion and Helen was pleased she wanted to do something. Lately her brooding depression had strained their closeness.

The bar served late and they were enjoying themselves, talking to other women and dancing, so that they almost missed the last bus. Helen, away from the warmth and the atmosphere's stimulus, felt drained. Walking up the road, her pace slowed down. Rats was drunk, swaying slightly as she walked and, though she was concerned, she was not a very practical support when Helen needed to lean against her for the final stretch up Caitlin Road.

The street was far from deserted. People were walking dogs even at this late hour. There were groups like themselves coming home from nights out, a constant stream of men to and from the synagogue. Helen and Rats weaved their unsteady way through this late night activity and took their leave of Brenda to the sound of a high wind, starting to shake down the leaves.

As they approached their flat, Rats put her hand into her pocket for the key. She couldn't find it and stood still going through all her pockets in turn, starting to walk back peering at the ground. 'Did you hear anything? I must have dropped it.'

Helen sat down on a low wall. She was desperate for her bed, she had pushed herself too far today. She felt like crying for the nearness of the flat, the lost key. Rats had gone a good way back down the road and Helen felt suddenly nervous. She had never been still on the streets at night before, always moving, making the distance between where she was and needed to be as short as possible. Rats was walking back to her, staggering slightly every once in a while. She looked funny and Helen called out playfully. 'Come on you drunkard. Where's this key then? It's too cold for the park bench, you know. Get a move on.'

Rats just carried on walking. When she got to Helen she sat down on the wall too, 'I can't find it. I've lost it. I don't know what to do.'

Helen put her arm round her and drew her to her. 'We'll think of something.'

As she spoke, she remembered the key going into her purse for safe-keeping while Rats had been dancing with Brenda. She brought it out, the key was still there. Rats could have kissed her, and she did, a long, slow, kiss anticipating the pleasures of the bed they might have been denied. A car door slammed twice though there had been no noise of an engine.

Rats and Helen, arms round each other, walked towards their flat and straight into trouble. Two men blocked their way. As they moved out into the road to pass them, they moved too; as they moved back, so did the men.

'Look what we've got here, John.'

'Shall we do them a favour, eh? Give 'em a bit of the real stuff?'

'Don't like the look of it, you can see why they've got each other. No man would want a go at that.'

As they spoke, the men dodged and weaved about, blocking possible escape routes, darting at them, threatening to touch or grab them. Rats and Helen, caught off guard, stood side by side, trying to turn their fear to anger. They were standing by their own gate, yet they felt far, far from home.

Voices behind the men distracted them. Helen saw a group of five Hassidims approaching, strung out along the pavement, walking quickly, talking animatedly. She touched Rats' arm and they rushed at the two men, who slipped and punched at them but did not manage to restrain them. Rats and Helen made it inside their door, a fresh string of insults ringing in their ears.

Helen slipped to the floor in the entrance hall, the effort of running and the tension had finished her. Rats was shaking all over. It took them a while to get upstairs. Helen lay down on the bed while Rats made tea. She laced her own with whiskey, weighing for a moment Helen's alcohol ban with the state of distress she was in. She decided not to risk it and sugared her tea instead.

'They know where we live now. We should have just run off and come back later, but I couldn't have gone another step. And they might have followed us.'

'Helen, one of those men had a lisp didn't he, and a scar?'

'Yes, look you're not going to suggest we go to the police. They won't take it seriously, even if they'd assaulted us, raped us, they wouldn't be that sympathetic. Women out on the streets, especially if

106

they've been drinking, should know better. And lesbians are just getting what they deserve, or secretly want. The police wouldn't listen to us.'

'It's not that. I know him, I saw him today. I saw him at Pershing's.'

The tea had revived Helen, briefly. Now the waves of exhaustion were rolling back, making her body heavy, straining her eyes to keep them open, thickening her tongue. She could do without Pershing at this stage. 'Rats, maybe you're just reacting badly to this, it was dark. You couldn't see that clearly.'

Hysteria sent Rats voice high, she was almost screaming.

'Helen, I saw him. We could see their faces, I heard his voice. Why don't you believe me, you don't know what it's like. I think I'm going mad. All these things happening, they're all linked to Pershing, they are. It's bad enough they happen, but when no one believes you, well, I must be insane, I must be making it all up.'

Rats sat on the edge of the bed sobbing. Helen barely had the energy to comfort her. They were both on edge, too wound up to sleep, too tired to talk. Helen got Rats to lie down and gently rocked her, soothing herself too. She whispered in her ear, words to reassure and calm her, until she lay still, both of them crying. 'Tomorrow,' she said, 'we'll talk tomorrow. We're safe now.'

Getting undressed and hurrying under the covers, they tried desperately to feel that safety. But knowing that the men had seen them come into this house, perhaps waited to see which light came on, undermined their security. They were as vulnerable here, as defenceless, as they were on the streets of the city.

The next day they slept late. Rats made breakfast in bed for them both, well past lunchtime. They were both very careful with each other, giving and expressing their pleasure in the smallest of things done. Outside, the sky was darkening with threatened rain, the trees were being stripped before their eyes.

'Let's stay in bed, all day.'

'We can't do that. It's all right for you, being an invalid but I ought to make some kind of effort.'

Helen ran her fingers down Rats' back. 'What sort of an effort had you in mind?' she said, tempting her back under the covers.

Later, lying together, their feet interleaved like children playing pat-a-cake, they found it possible to talk about the incident with the two men. They were both scared, disturbed that the men knew where they lived. But Rats returned endlessly to the man she recognised, slotting this event in with the others surrounding Pershing. Her fear opened depths of insecurity in her, lost her any perspective on what had happened. Helen's fear fuelled her anger. They talked, but without any resolution.

Suddenly the door bell rang, making them both jump. Visitors at the flat were rare, it was too late in the day for the post or a meter reading: Rats wanted to ignore it, but their caller was insistent. Helen was curious.

'Go and see who it is. The light's on, we're obviously in.'

'What if it's them, those men? Just leave it, they'll go.'

But the doorbell rang again, this time continuously. Helen got up, reaching for a dressing gown and went towards the door. It seemed an effort for her. Rats responded by getting up, taking the dressing gown and going herself.

She paused before the door, trying to make out the shape on the other side. At least there was only one as far as she could see. Opening the door she saw a woman she vaguely recognised holding Dusty in a towel. 'Hello, I've brought your cat back, he is yours isn't he? I think he's been hit by a car, he was in my garden. There's a lot of blood and his back legs look smashed up.'

Rats reached out to stroke her cat. As she did so she heard again Pershing's voice, lazily describing cats' deaths to her. In her relief at Dusty's return she could acknowledge the silent fear she had had that Pershing had somehow been responsible for his absence. Dusty was very still, his eyes full of pain; feebly he licked her hand while Rats mustered a response to her neighbour.

'Thank you, come in. This is terrible, he's been missing a few days. I'll have to get him to a vet.'

'If you want I'll take you round in my car. Do you want to get dressed? I'll wait here with him.'

Rats went up stairs to explain to Helen, her distress over Dusty's accident competing with her relief that it was not the men.

While Rats was out, Helen thought some more about her obsession with Pershing. It worried her, not in the same way Pershing worried Rats. He wasn't a sinister figure to Helen, but she was concerned by the way Rats seemed to bring everything back to him; it verged on paranoia and it certainly wasn't doing her any good. Helen realised that telling Rats to forget it, put it behind her, wasn't going to work.

She had always been stubborn and this was no exception. It seemed to Helen that Rats' obsession fed on her lack of knowledge; in the absence of hard facts it was easy to slide everything and anything into a world view dominated by Pershing as a dangerous scheming man, covering his tracks. If that body had been there, and Helen sometimes found herself doubting it had, then it was clearly murder. The only way to try to rid Rats of her fear was to try and find out what had happened.

Dusty was the centre of attention when they returned. His pelvis was broken and he had to be kept still, so they settled him into a corner of the room. After they had eaten, Helen suggested her idea. At first Rats was reluctant, she didn't think they could do anything, it scared her. Helen cajoled, it would at least keep them occupied, allow them to do something with the anger and fear they both felt.

They listed all the incidents since Rats had come across the body in Pershing's car. Helen was smiling as she finished. 'Everything and nothing, isn't it?'

'There was the man in the cemetery as well.'

'Do you think that was connected?'

'I suppose I do. It's a strange thing that's happened to me recently, anyway. That's true of the rest of it.'

Helen shrugged. She thought the incident owed more to Rats' imagination than anything else. She didn't doubt that it had happened, but was reluctant to include it. Rats was persistent.

'The tramp spoke to me, he said he'd seen me.'

Helen wasn't going to push it.

'Okay then, but it could have meant anything.'

They sat looking at the list, waiting for it to make some sense, for an order to emerge. Rats giggled. Helen looked over at her, wary of the hysteria only just in check. She needn't have worried, Rats was not hysterical. Eventually she managed to speak. 'We're like Miss Marple or Jemima Shore. All set to ferret out the truth, bring wrongdoers to justice.'

Helen giggled with her. 'What a laugh. Do you think they ever sat around like this, waiting for things to come together? For the next chapter to be written? I wish I knew what to do next.'

'Make a cup of tea.'

Throughout the evening, cups of tea were resorted to along with cigarettes and biscuits. They established that whatever mystery they had stumbled into, it concerned Pershing's business. They would need to find out more about it. They weren't sure where to begin.

Rats had been brought up respecting the public library – she saw it as the repository of all wisdom and information. She thought they should ask at a library. Behind her faith stood years of killing time on winter evenings after school, doing homework in the reference library rather than struggling to find a quiet spot in her boisterous, crowded home. She retained her child's faith in the power of the library to unravel the complexities of books and the knowledge they contained. Helen was less convinced. She doubted that they would ever get within reach of any knowledge worth having, or that if they did, they could make anything of it. She wanted to start with what they knew, what Rats remembered.

They listed the different companies and branches of business that Rats recalled from Lindy's. Some she was fairly certain were part of a larger company, owned by Pershing but managed on franchise or leased to various managers. Others had a more complex relationship that she was not clear about. They listed the names and, where she could remember, the addresses.

'It's probably just a tax fiddle, well within the law,' Helen commented as she looked over the little cluster of estate agents, insurance companies and property agencies spread out now over three pages of the writing pad.

'But why worry about it then, and why kill?'

'We don't know the death had anything to do with the business. We don't actually know the death happened or that it was Pershing's car. You might have mistaken it. After all, it was a shock. The mind plays funny tricks sometimes.'

'Helen!' Rats was angry now, her eyes dry, no suspicion of tears. 'That death is the only thing that makes all this hang together. Take that away and it's just your averagely seedy, pushing on hard times, dubious outfit. I don't like the business, but it's not illegal. I might wish we all had a decent place to live, as of right. But we don't. And as long as we don't there'll be places like Lindy's, feeding on need, making their money. I don't like it, but it's not a crime. Same goes for the insurance sharks and the rest of it. There has to be something else. That something else is the killing.'

'But we don't know that. As far as I know – actually know – you're the only person who ever saw it, it's only your word that it was Pershing's car, you're word that he's awkward with you, that it got worse once he knew where you lived. That it's because he guessed you knew about the body and the car.'

'And my word isn't good enough? Isn't to be trusted?'

'I didn't say that.'

'Didn't need to.'

'There are other things as well. It interests me that he was running a company that as far as I can make out did no trading. Then he closes it down. It doesn't seem to me that he suddenly realised it wasn't profitable. That's more of a puzzle to me. More seems to lie behind a decision like that, especially seeing as he's involved in so many other companies. I wonder how many other places are being opened up and closed down, and why.'

'I saw that body. And I know the car. I don't need you telling me I imagined it. It was real, still is. I've been through doubting my own sanity far more thoroughly than you ever could. I know what I saw. I want to know why too.'

'It may all be linked. We need to start looking for information, deciding what to look for, where.'

'How do we begin? Where do we start? Would there be court reports? Just in case the body was found and it went to court.'

'We need to start with coroners' reports for that, the register of deaths. If it went to court or not, it still has to be registered as a death. That's the first stage. With the company I need to look through a register, try to sort out who exactly owns what. Perhaps we could just start by doing that, trying to find out something, then see what it looks like.'

21

Over the next few weeks they each pursued their own strands. It was not easy. Not knowing exactly what they were looking for or whether they had any right of access to the information, they were often clumsy in their approach to officials. Such clumsiness and lack of confidence was treated with suspicion, people were less helpful than they might have been, more obstructive in any case, than was their normal response to such enquiries.

Rats did start her search in the public libraries, in the small room at the back with old-fashioned wooden tables and chairs set out in rows, in amongst the people killing time with the magazines, the newly unemployed sifting them for situations vacant, the others casting bored eyes over block after block of print. While students at the local college wrote or sat dreaming over essays for their exams, Rats studied all the local press dating from the night she had seen the body.

She was looking for a report of the death, a court report, a coroner's inquest. She didn't find the one she was looking for but over the days she felt herself dragged down by the weight of other people's loss and grieving. From January through to April, there were numerous suicides – people of all ages, often unemployed, often with histories of psychiatric illness. With each name, and its own particular route into obscurity etched into a column of newsprint, Rats was reminded how close to that line she and Helen had come. They were the lucky ones, with something – she didn't know what it was – to sustain them through the tangle of severed connections, the absence of useful activity, the diminishing of hope. Rats was grateful for Helen, for her support and encouragement, her presence. Without each other, they would be as cut loose, drifting down, as any of these routine tragedies.

Most of the cases took up very little space. There was usually a short notice at the time of the incident, perhaps two or three sentences. If there had been something obviously newsworthy – a jump from a high building, a leap under a train, preferably with shocked witnesses to interview – this would extend to a few paragraphs. Some time later, the usual time was about three months, there would follow the inquest report. Just a line or two giving the verdict unless something singled it out: allegations of negligence, or some circumstance such as bad housing or unemployment that was being trawled through the paper as a rallying point for social concern. Rats found these painful to read. As she came up to date with the weeks she was searching, she was still no clearer about the body in the car. She had decided that the word suicide, taking one's own life, was wrong. It did not adequately describe the process she had seen, however patchily and briefly laid out before her. It was a different form of murder, she thought – the suicide just disposed of the husk that someone else had stolen the life from long before.

Flicking through the pages of the papers in front of her she thought local papers must be the worst way to learn about an area, a distillation

112

of all that is lowest and meanest, the pettiest of petty crime. And all bulked out with pages and pages of things to sell – houses, cars, services, jobs, as if the whole of life was simply a series of cash exchanges. And between this, the momentary puffs of fame for the street festivals, the playgroup that received a royal visit. What a life.

She stopped at a page in April. The coroner's inquest into a joint suicide had merited most of an inside page. The man had lived in the area although the suicide had taken place in Epping Forest. She looked at the photos. An attractive woman in her late twenties. Why did photos always show people smiling for the camera, as she did, conscious of how pretty she looked? Susan Tinsley and George Horrocks smiled out at her. The two photos had probably been taken long before they met. They had been lovers. What had driven them to that sordid end under the trees in Epping? Rats learned very little from the report. She wondered, for instance, who had decided to shoot the other and then themselves? Probably the man, George, it was a male thing to do. Susan looked as if she might be one of those women unused to machines, clumsy through her fear of them. Rats looked a moment longer at these hopeful smiling faces. Then she closed the paper and took her pile of them back to the counter.

Rats needed some relief from these catalogues of death she had been picking over for the last few weeks. She and Helen had only cursorily compared notes each night and the investigations were less important than their usual activities together of spending time watching TV, reading, chatting about this and that. Perhaps this weekend they should compare notes.

Food seemed a good way to remind herself she was in the land of the living. There was a cafe across the way, run as a work experience scheme or a co-op, she wasn't sure which. The food was reasonably priced and there were generous helpings. Just the thing for a cold day. Rats chose Toad in the Hole and it came with potatoes, cabbage and cauliflower, smothered in rich, thick gravy. As she started to eat, she noticed a young woman come in, stumbling over her order at the counter. She seemed unable to make her mind up, then having decided, had opted for a meal not in fact on the menu. She wavered in embarrassment, looked around and Rats felt her eyes rest on her plate. She ordered Toad in the Hole, then came and sat at the table, warming her hands on her mug.

Nothing was said, but her body conveyed the strain of needing to talk, wanting to make contact. Rats saw all that and decided to ignore it. She didn't smile or make an opening remark, knowing that the girl was too nervous to initiate anything. She ate through her meal as if the space across the table from her was still empty. The girl looked as if this was nothing more than she might have expected. Rats felt guilty, but didn't waver. Her head was too full of the wreckage of their times to be able to offer any comfort to someone headed, she imagined, for her own rocky groundings. She didn't linger over her meal, paying the price later with indigestion.

Helen, still recovering from her illness, had worked more slowly. She had gone with Rats to the public library and been surprised that the young woman there did indeed know where she should begin to look up the ownership of certain companies. The directory didn't actually list any of the firms known to Rats and Helen, but all the same it was useful to have learned her way around it, listing as it did, directors, share capital and subsidiary firms. Once she had established that none of her companies were there, Helen turned to some of the better known firms; she looked up banks and building societies, retail stores, food manufacturers. The amount of money listed as share capital amazed her. Row after row of noughts. And the employees, listed as figures, just as they were in the unemployment statistics. She was surprised by how many of the big companies owned equally big companies often dealing in financial services of one kind or another. Money makes money makes money, thought Helen as she sat deciding what to do next.

Over the next few days she took trade directories from the shelves and worked through them. She found some of the firms listed but it told her nothing. She went back to the woman at the counter to ask her advice. Most of the directories were put together by advertisers or professional associations; she would need to go to Companies House if she wanted to take her enquiries further. Once there, the commissionaire passed her through, having first phoned what Helen imagined was a public relations office of some sort. She was directed to the third floor.

Room 326 was an above averagely furnished ante-room, where a woman in her forties was waiting. Helen introduced herself as a student on the business studies course at City and East London College. She began to explain her project. The woman described the nature of access to the information held there which, on the whole, seemed to be an account of lack of access. Eventually, however,

Helen was asked which companies she required information on and asked to return at 11.30 the following Thursday.

As she walked back to the lift she decided to take a look around. She walked along the corridor past closed doors from which came the sound of voices, sometimes activity. The whole floor seemed to be a canteen and rest area. There was little to interest her here. She found the emergency stairs and went up to the next floor. The signs on the doors meant little to her, she walked about, hovered in front of a few doors then proceeded on to the next floor. By the sixth floor her calf muscles were weakening and she was starting to wonder exactly why she was creeping about the building. She didn't know what she expected to find or how she would recognise it if she did stumble across it. Gratefully she called the lift and took it down to the ground floor. As she waited for a bus home, she decided the powerlessness of those like herself lay in not knowing the ground rules of the opposition, knowing only that they kept one step ahead and probably made it up as they went along.

Helen spent the time before her appointment following up a different range of enquiries, those generally concerned with housing. She concentrated on Shelter and Shac and the smaller housing pressure groups. They all had interesting, lively programmes of events and seemed keen for her to become actively involved. She held back from these offers, though they tempted her. She was still feeling the effects of her illness, the investigation put a strain on her and yet she felt an obligation to Rats to keep it up. At the same time, though, she was beginning to feel the need for a life apart from Rats, to make her own friends, establish some sort of activity and involvement for herself independently.

At Helen's appointment at Companies House she learnt something, but nothing very much about Pershing's companies. As she had begun to suspect, many of the smaller ones were simply partnerships and not registered. The parent company existed under a number of names, which seemed to change at fairly regular intervals. There were three directors and a variety of addresses which cropped up regularly. Helen made a note of these, noting too that accounts hadn't been filed as required. One of the addresses was on Stamford Hill, just after the turning for Caitlin Road. As she wrote it down, Helen saw that it explained what Pershing's car might have been doing there, but nothing explained the mysterious body in it. There was nothing here that she hadn't already guessed at. Plainly, if the pursuit of the company was going to come to anything she would have to try and find a different angle to approach it all from.

That Friday night they decided to eat out. They chatted over the meal about their findings. The atmosphere between them was relaxed, they each had activity to report, but no conclusions. Any kind of understanding of what was going on at Pershing's seemed a long way off. It was as if each wanted to carry on their search, but would be happy to let the other persuade them out of it. They were still wavering when they paid the bill and decided to go for a drink.

Over a drink they agreed to continue the enquiries a little longer. Rats would see whether the coroner's reports were available to consult, or the registry of deaths, and Helen would see whether any of the housing action groups she'd come across would be able to help pin down something on Pershing. Rats wanted to swop, or work together; she was finding the study of death depressing. Now, as in the weeks immediately after her discovery of the body, life all around was reduced to its end. Rats shivered. Helen told her she should see it through, it was not for her to take over at this stage.

Helen for her part was excited at the prospect of learning more about the different groups. Perhaps getting actively involved with them. She remembered a TV programme from way back. A woman on a railway platform, a couple of children and tears. All the weight of that woman's despair flickering in black and white and a silence, then her dad stretching, saying, 'How about a brew up, Mother?' and her mother saying, 'Sssh, I want to watch this,' and herself sitting awkward, bored, feeling she should squeeze some tears out in sympathy with those of her mother's, and her father's little clicks of disgust. 'It's over,' her father had said, prodding her mother, 'that's it.' The credits were, indeed, rolling over the figure. There was still no sound. Helen's mother had got up and gone into the kitchen.

Since then Helen had been aware throughout the seventies of the various issues and campaigns around housing, but it had never been central to her. The politics of housing had been about families, excluding her as a lesbian. But here in London Helen was gaining a different sense of the importance of housing and beginning to see the possibility of taking part in a struggle over it. Pershing was only part of the picture.

However close to the wind Pershing might swing, he was always able to keep on the right side of the law. The law was on his side. The law said it was better to be a slum landlord than a slum tenant, morally superior and infinitely more profitable; that the need to own property was to be satisfied over and above the need to put a roof over your head. Helen was impatient to find a way of tackling Pershing. Talking to Rats though, she didn't feel her enthusiasm reciprocated. For Rats, it was all very personal with Pershing, ultimately to do with the death. She didn't appreciate Helen's urge to take things further, to widen the scope of what they were doing. Rats thought it presumptuous of them, to think they alone could intervene and affect the path of a man as powerful as Pershing.

As Helen moved towards new departures and a changed sense of the problems they confronted, Rats was ground further down into the morass of the old. She had been allowed to see the register of deaths, saying she was researching infant mortality as part of a post-qualification certificate in nursing. The sheer number each day shocked Rats, then the random causes, the age range. Nothing seemed secure, and there was nothing to compensate her for the terror induced by the search, no male in his late thirties meeting a violent end in January. Only the suicide, again, and six deaths from multiple injuries that, she imagined, were caused by car crashes or fights. She had to give up. Helen was worried about her, had been woken by her nightmares, her mutterings and screams in the night. However, Helen continued to attend her meetings, read reports and minutes. She was out a lot of the time which she felt vaguely uneasy about, knowing how vulnerable Rats was feeling. But she had to go to meetings and Rats could have come with her, but she wouldn't. So, as that week merged into the next, Rats and Helen spent less and less time together, and Rats' fear of death grew large and more powerful, moving from sleep into the edges of her waking life.

22

On Sunday they took their chances on the yellowing grey sky and went out for a walk. They were standing on the bridge over the Lea when Rats, startled by Helen's hand on her shoulder, suddenly began to cry. Not her usual tears of pride and self-pity, but tears that made her chest and shoulders heave, her sobs audible. Helen held her close, then started to walk her back towards the park and a bench. Once there she sat beside her, holding her hand while Rats sobbed on, burying her head in Helen's shoulder.

After a while Rats was able to tell her she had glimpsed a large branch, borne downstream with the current and momentarily confused it with a body. This reminded her of the body she had seen drifting down this very river. Now her fear was that whoever killed the body in the car would strike again. It didn't matter that they had killed for no apparent reason. To Rats this only made it more likely they would do it again. All that mattered was that they had got away with it. It was almost an encouragement to them, sobbed Rats, in the grip of panic.

Helen tried to keep her comments general, calming. Rats' tears finally stopped, her shivers now because of the cold air. Helen suggested that they went back to the flat. Once there, she persuaded Rats to lie on the bed and rest while she made tea. Rats slept, exhausted by the cold and the strain.

When she woke, Rats appeared calmer but was more entrenched in her fears. The logical way she described her terror and its causes worried Helen more than her panic had. Finding out who had killed the body in the car was no longer about settling scores with the past, it was for the future. Killing was a thing that could be, would be repeated. Helen was silenced. She didn't know what to suggest. The whole thing lurched between housing and death, the known and the unknown. It was going to have to come down somewhere, between fear of the imagined and the real.

That night when they talked, Rats kept coming back to the man in the cemetery. Helen couldn't understand why he seemed so central to Rats. She didn't think there was anything he could explain to her. But Rats was adamant, said the men who pursued her then must have been the same ones who had gone to Plaistow and Mare Street looking for her. Helen didn't risk contradicting this, though she was sceptical that the men were the same. Realising Rats' concern with the death had gone beyond rationality, Helen humoured her. She agreed to go tomorrow with Rats to search the cemetery for him. She felt sure he would have left the cemetery now for warmer winter stopping places.

As she lay awake that night, Rats thought of contacting the police. She had the same reluctance to involve them as on that first night.

But she felt that they, unlike the rest of us, knew how to deal with death. They were the ones who broke down the doors harbouring neglected, long dead old-age pensioners; they were the ones to sort the flesh from metal in motorway pile-ups. Her desire was stronger than her unease about the parts they played in some other deaths and her own mistrust of them. She was not to know that there was a procedure for letters such as hers, a procedure that meant it would not be investigated.

The next day they left the house about eleven. Rats was silent. Helen too felt weighed down. It was drizzling, the rain had a cold edge to it. Day by day, winter was coming on. As they walked, heads down against the windy rain, they discussed how to search. Ordinarily they might have split up, but today Helen needed to be close to Rats. Inside Abney Park, the trees were almost bare. There were still some swatches of greenery but the plants, lush and extensive as they had been, were dying back. A local conservation group had been clearing the graves, but only near the entrances. Further on the density of the overgrowth made the cemetery seem impenetrable, creating the illusion that it covered more ground than it did.

They walked deep into the heart of the park. Radiating out from the main avenues were paths that began clear enough, but narrowed down to a dense, twigged tangle, the green merging into black, light blocked out. Neither woman was anxious to push down through these paths although they knew that if the man was here, they were unlikely to come across him on the main thoroughways.

They agreed to start at his hideout and work their way around. Rats wasn't exactly sure where it was, but felt confident that she would recognise it again. That day had been so unreal, the fear of the place concentrated in the steady tread of footsteps behind her, and then the desire to run, to get away and that final, almost surreal, relief with the tramp and his hidey hole. Rats remembered how unlike her idea of a tramp he had been.

They went in the direction she recalled and came to a halt outside the structure she thought she recognised. They called out, embarrassed by their own voices interrupting the silence. Nothing stirred, there was not even that artificial quiet as if someone were holding their breath, maintaining cover, to delay discovery. Rats knew she could try to open up the hidey hole but was reluctant to do so. It seemed clear he wasn't there.

119

They decided to fan out and explore further, walking briskly along those paths that were reasonably good underfoot. They carried on half-hoping, half-expecting to meet the man. They were disappointed. Finding themselves at the old church, its windows boarded up, graffiti sprayed along its walls, an arc of unexplored paths off to the left, the entrance gates ahead, they sheltered against the church wall.

'He's not here, is he?'

'No. I wonder, would he move on, for the winter? It's hard to tell. I guess he would.'

'Should we try the rest of the park?'

'Hardly seems worth it. I'm frozen.'

They were both buffing their arms and jigging about for warmth. As they walked back towards the entrance, Helen broached the topic that depressed her just as much as the cold and the damp. 'If he really has gone, what then?' She walked, no answer came, she continued. 'We're not going to be able to pin him down at all. What are we going to do?'

Rats was thoughtful. The activity of searching had seemed to steady her. But the future was still there, shadowed for them both by the need to lay the ghost of the body in the car. For today, Rats was prepared to leave it, but she wanted them both to go back tomorrow to search the remaining paths.

The next day found them walking side by side through the backways of the park. They were blind to its charms, ghosted by the mist of early rain and the dying flourishes of autumn. A damp autumn, no flash of fire hanging evocatively over the trees and scrubby borders. The day held no real promise for either of them. They had squabbled in the morning over whether or not to go out. And the squabble had another focus in the meeting Helen was going to that evening. She had decided to join a local housing action group. It was a small group, not linked with the big national campaigns, and made up mostly of people at the sharp end of the area's shortcomings in housing. Helen had found a place for herself there, begun to make friends. There were some young homeless people who had resorted to squatting, some council tenants impatient of ever-lengthening transfer lists and delays over basic repairs, there were a few tenants in private rented places. There were no owner-occupiers and there was a tacit agreement to exclude them.

Helen wanted Rats to come with her, to throw in her lot with that slower struggle. Rats was dogged in her determination not to be sidetracked from the pursuit of Pershing and the unravelling of the mystery of his car and its body. After their quarrel, they had reached a sullen compromise: Helen would go with Rats to the graveyard, Rats would go with Helen to the meeting. In each case, it was a grudging gesture.

As they walked the graveyard paths, the atmosphere between them thickened. They hardly spoke, there was nothing, really, for them to say to each other. It was difficult, given the lie of the land, to know when they had covered all the areas they could, whether they weren't just going over the same ground. Helen held back from calling a halt. It was important that Rats say it, admit the failure of the search and in doing so, its folly. Rats kept walking, setting the pace. She could not admit defeat, too much hung on that. She imagined, for a moment, walking on and on until forced to stop, her feet worn out, throat parched. She saw, in a glimpse of panic, the park as a maze, endless paths, endless openings. Saw the entrance fade further and further from view. So they continued for another hour until Helen could hold her tongue no longer. 'It's no good. We've got to stop this.'

They came to a halt. Rats picked one or two blackberries from a forgotten cache. Once rich and heavy, they now had a sharp bitterness, a woody taste, already returning to the earth, past their best. They absorbed her as Helen's voice did not.

'Rats, listen to me. I'm going back. This is foolish. He's not here, if he ever was, if it makes any difference whether he was or not.'

She had said too much. Rats still did not speak, but merely turned away from her and began to retrace her steps. Helen followed her. She was not inclined to try and repair the damage that had been done between them, not just today but over the last few weeks. Why should she be the one to placate, to back down? She did not know what Rats was thinking, had to admit that she did not much care.

When they reached the main road she was tempted to simply get on a bus, go into a shop, leave her. She couldn't stand the stoic, silent face, the grim taking upon herself of sorrow. Let her suffer, she thought, let her stew in her own bloody juices. She sat on a bench. She saw Rats hesitate as she realised Helen was no longer tagging along behind. Rats had her pride too, she got as far as the other side of the road before she stopped properly, turned round and looked back. Waiting. Helen looked across at her, then looked down. Let her wait.

Next time Helen looked it was to see her figure retreating. Helen got up and followed her down the road. In the end there was no evading it, they would have to have it out.

As she left, the bench was taken over by a group of grubby and tattered men holding close their bottles of cider and sherry. But there was one slightly out of place, whose fingernails, had you been close enough to see them, were clean and rested neatly at the tips of his fingers, raw in their pinkness.

When Helen neared home she found her resolve to straighten things out one way or another had left her. She carried on walking up to the Clapton Road, crossed over and waited for a bus. As she climbed aboard she had no clear idea of where she was going. The bus said 'Aldgate'. Aldgate, the way she felt, was fine. She paid her fare and sat back as the bus moved slowly through Hackney, then Bethnal Green. She watched it empty, then fill up, then empty again. She got off at Aldgate and bought herself a tub of cockles from the stall at the end of the street. There wasn't a lot to walk around and look at. A huge six-lane roundabout took up most of the space. Small dress factories, workrooms really, were crowded into the buildings lining the small lanes that ran behind the main High Street. She wandered into an Art Gallery. It was a clear, light building, painted white, the floor smooth pale wood. The exhibits confused her; she picked her way among them, wondering how it was possible to distinguish one pile of rubble, metal and plastic from another. Outside there was a steady thrum of traffic. She wondered whether she could spend the rest of the day away from the flat.

She walked back up Whitechapel High Street, stopping every now and then to look over some item on the stalls that ran the length of the street. There were only a few hours before the meeting began. Helen decided to stay out, she couldn't face Rats, needed time to sort out how she felt. The weight of the last few weeks was telling upon them, Helen needed to ease up the pressure on her life. She needed time to think.

The meeting, when she finally got to it at seven o'clock, had nothing to mark it as out of the ordinary. But for Helen it was a watershed; Rats wasn't there and she began to think that maybe this was just the first of a long series of places and times that Rats wasn't going to be there. Being new to the group she had plenty of opportunity to sit back and think. She was introduced to them all but could remember only three or four of the names. There were about ten of them. There was no pressure on her to join in, volunteer, but at the same time she didn't feel left out. The meeting started to break up at about nine o'clock. Most of them were going on to a pub; only Jackie, who she knew had children, was going straight home. Helen felt she too had responsibilities at home and declined the invitations. Christine wrote the date and place of the next meeting on a piece of paper for her. 'Try and get your friend to come along, we can always use some more help.'

Helen paused outside the street door, wishing that she had the false courage of drink and the memory of companionable friendliness in the pub. The light was on in the flat. The silence magnified her every sound, it made her clumsy. She dropped keys, clattered up the stairs, stumbled coming into the flat, clattered the kettle. There was no greeting, but she could sense Rats lying there, awake and listening.

'Want a coffee?'

No sound. She made her own and walked through to the bedroom. Rats lay on her side, the cover pulled over her ears, the pillows pulled down. Helen could almost feel how tightly squeezed shut she was keeping her eyes. She sat down on the bed, put her coffee on the bedside table and kicked her shoes off. They spent the night together keeping the space in the middle of the bed between them.

They spoke in the morning as they continued to speak in the coming days. Exchanges of information, requests to be included in, or out, of meals, shopping, housework. They did not squabble over the minor irritations of life together, nor reproach each other's late nights, or heap recriminations from the uncomfortable, cold corners of their life together. They didn't speak about that night or about the day that had led up to it. The papers they had collected together, their notes, lay on the table, gathering dust. It continued like this for three weeks. Although no anger, or sadness, was expressed it was there. They could have gone on for months. Silent, separate but unwilling to sever connections, powerless to rescue some comfort for themselves out of their failure to live with and provide for each other. The row, when it came, was as predictable as its resolution. The door slamming and the irretrievable steps down the road. The leaving. It was Helen who went, to her new friends. The sound of people passing under the window echoed into the night until Rats could no longer keep the memory of Helen's footsteps separate from all the others.

23

Alone, Rats' first feeling was of relief, then a rush of guilt. But the relief surfaced again. She couldn't pin it down, it was a sense of freedom and restlessnes. She went out to the off licence and bought some beer as much for the walk as anything. Back in the flat she started to pack Helen's things. It was a satisfying task, combining activity with a symbolic power. It was a way of testing herself, her resistance, her ability to cope and organise herself. With that done, Rats cooked herself a meal, opened a can of beer and settled back to watch TV. Her elation was shortlived. By the following evening she had begun to grieve, found herself unable to stop crying. She felt the emptiness of their small flat echo about her, loneliness bouncing off its walls and catching her off guard. She went to bed early, a sense of desolation weighing her down.

The next week passed in a haze for Rats; her head was thick, as if it ached permanently, she moved slowly, exhausted by the simplest physical exertion. Her hair was greasy, her skin more grey than pink, unwashed and unhealthy. She found choosing clothes unbearable and clung to the comfort of an old brushed cotton shirt and her brown cord jeans. She wore them day in day out. They needed washing. She was sweating heavily, despite the cold and her shirt quickly took on a sharp, acidy smell. The weekend lay like a life sentence. The streets around were busy and their activity diminished her further. The crowds were made up of smartly dressed Jewish women with their daughters and men-folk, celebrating Channuka, but Rats was not to know that. She realised only that women were a part of the coming and going, whereas usually it was the men and boys who made this street their own.

For Rats, the festivity emphasised her difference, her isolation, to see family groups, parties of friends and neighbours out in their best clothes, with their children. She looked out of her window at the procession of prams, neat pastel coloured frocks, the white tights. She stood for a while, pacing the small length of her front room, her mind seemingly blank but constantly picking over fragments of speech, recollected images, memory or imagination. She took off her clothes

124

and got into bed. It was a little after seven on a Saturday night. She stayed there until Monday evening.

Groggy with too much sleep, sick and sorry for herself, she took a shower and washed her hair. She found a clean nightie and put it on, along with her slippers and a dressing gown. She swallowed two aspirins, remembering Auntie Maude's belief that there wasn't a thing in the world that couldn't be put to rights by aspirin and a strong cup of tea. Half closing her eyes, she saw the worn floral print pinny over a shapeless, colourless dress, thick-stockinged legs stuck into worn carpet slippers. Maude was long dead, past the benison of tea and aspirin. Maude and the thousands of women like her would not be helpless as she was. It was as if generations of the women of her family crowded into that room, peasant women, wives of farm labourers, mill girls, servants, factory lasses. And the spirit of putting up with the world, getting by, was distilled down into its bitter cup. As bitter as the taste of aspirin dissolving on her tongue. Rats began to believe in the possibility of her recovery, her own strength. She made tea for herself and took it back to bed. Her sleep that night was peaceful. The cat purred against her long into the night and the shadows on the wall did not trouble her.

She woke refreshed. Smartly dressed in clean clothes, she set out to do the rounds of the job centre, the employment agencies and the classified ads in the local paper. Rats felt it was important to work. All her life the people around her had worked, at hard jobs, with long hours, that took their toll of them. To live was to work, for her, she felt out of touch with herself out of work. She had enough experience now though, not to stake everything on getting a job. She was prepared to be disappointed – which was just as well because she was to receive over the next few days a resounding no, nothing doing, not suitable, I'm afraid all the vacancies have gone, from everything she went after. She wondered for a while whether work as such existed. Whether the whole city wasn't colluding in its absence, whether in fact anyone did go out to work. But some of the shops were busy and surely all the check-outs couldn't be staffed by young women on YTS schemes. And the crowds pouring through those aisles with their loaded trolleys were spending money that came from somewhere. Not the dole, that's for sure. The week dragged into two.

Helen's belongings were still stacked in a corner of the bedroom. Rats was past the stage of seeing her in everyone she glimpsed in the crowd. She wondered, eventually, whether Helen had left London. She had never taken to it in the way Rats had. It was difficult to believe she had just walked out like that, letting the time elapse with no word of her whereabouts. Sometimes in the nights of panic, Rats dreamt about Helen pursued by Pershing. She was always a helpless onlooker, screaming silently as Pershing turned aside from Helen to her, his face fading into the dead man's, his hands around her neck dripping blood. Although it would have been easy enough for Rats to contact Helen through the housing campaign she persisted in believing only Helen could contact her. Since Helen had left, she had evaded people, making excuses to Brenda and Liz whenever she bumped into them.

She was surprised, then, when the doorbell rang. Helen stood on the doorstep. They didn't speak for a few seconds. Rats pulled the door open: 'Come in, where's your key?'

'Here,' Helen held it in her hand, 'it seemed a bit rude just to barge in.'

They walked upstairs into the flat. Rats made coffee while Helen walked around the flat like a prospective buyer, as if the place was strange to her.

'You packed up my things.'

'Shouldn't I have?'

'Doesn't matter.'

'I thought you might have gone back up North.'

'No.'

They drank their coffee, fiddled with their empty mugs. 'Where are you staying?'

'With a friend. You don't know her.'

'Oh,' Rats felt a surge of jealousy, it showed in her face. It always did.

'I met her through the Housing Action Group. She's letting me sleep in her spare room. It's okay, but it's not permanent.'

'You still involved with that group then?'

'Yeah, I've been doing a lot with them. You never did come to that meeting.'

'No.'

'What've you been doing?'

'Not a lot.'

'Any news?' Helen indicated the pile of papers on the table. She noticed that they looked untouched.

'No.' Rats' 'no's' were delivered in a monotone. Helen knew her well enough to know there was more under the surface than she revealed. She kept up a string of questions, but Rats maintained her noncommittal replies until finally Helen was exasperated into silence.

'More coffee?'

'No, I'd like to talk to you.'

'I'm not stopping you, am I?'

'You aren't exactly encouraging. You haven't really answered a single question I've asked.'

'Perhaps I've nothing to say. Perhaps I've got a one-track mind, perhaps I'm only interested in one thing. Boring, dull, deadening to be with. Obsessed.'

Helen sat silent as she listened to the accusation she had undoubtedly laid at Rats' door. When Rats had finished, anger colouring her cheeks and her eyes glistening with tears unshed, Helen apologised.

She did so, restraining her own irritation at the way the argument was laid wholly on her shoulders, 'It was only that I was worried about you. I think you were too caught up with that death. It wasn't my obsession, I couldn't stand it any longer. Not you, I still love you. But you were taken over, I couldn't share that with you.'

'It's not finished for me, it's still there. It can't just end.'

Helen thought for a second Rats was talking about their relationship. With a sick feeling she realised it was not her but the death she meant. They fell silent again.

After a while Helen suggested going out for a drink, to the British Oak. In amongst the pool players and the couples they drank and talked, more relaxed now than earlier. They agreed to go on seeing each other, but there was an unstated, lesser commitment. In different ways, they were enjoying their independence.

Over the next few weeks they settled into a new routine, seeing each other two or three times a week, keeping separate interests but finding a new excitement in their relationship. Helen still tried to involve Rats with the housing campaign, Rats still brooded on the death.

Helen's campaign focused on the Council more than private landlords. Pershing's activities seemed less important than this systematic abuse of power, the glaring contradiction that their borough had 3,000 empty properties, 200 homeless families, not to mention the single homeless. And there were, as Marcella, Agnes, Steve and Desmond made sure the group didn't forget, the conditions under which Council tenants, the lucky ones, were housed.

Rats had come to a blank in her investigations. She felt her only hope lay in making contact with the tramp, but she didn't know how to do that. Vaguely she imagined that with spring he would return to the streets. She felt calm, as if she could wait. The urgency had gone, but there was no forgetting.

Rats' equilibrium wavered over the coming weeks. The search for a job demoralised her. She was increasingly nervous about the demands for rent from the landlords and the blank wall she encountered when trying to sort out her claim with the benefit office. Despite writing to her landlords, she continued to receive threatening letters. She despaired of ever making them understand that it was not deliberate. Perhaps she should pay rent out of her allowance, but that would leave her with only £4 a week to live on. She decided to try and send something, believing that if she showed willing it would appease them. She struggled and scraped by but the letters kept coming.

She discussed it with Helen who urged her to go to an advice centre or move out and live with her in a newly established squat. Helen and four others from the group had squatted the top floor of a thirties' block of council flats. Their existence there was just one more irony in the pattern of housing provision. The block had been refurbished two or three years previously, new windows, central heating, modern kitchen units. Then, the local Housing Committee decided that no children should be housed above the fifth floor. So, these two floors of two or three bedroomed flats had been offered to elderly, childless couples, the only category of applicants who had amassed enough points to be offered any accommodation. In every case the flats had been turned down because there was no lift in the block. So the flats remained empty until they were squatted by the young, single childless people who were only grudgingly admitted on to the housing waiting list and never gained sufficient points to be made an offer. There was a campaign to get all the flats occupied and then force the Council to accept rents and in so doing legalise the tenancies.

Helen was caught up in this new campaign and there seemed to be harmony between where she was living, her friends and the major preoccupation in her life. Rats felt pushed out. It wasn't that Helen didn't try to include her. Rats felt life was moving quickly for Helen; she could be part of those changes too but the pace was too quick. As

Helen became more and more exhilarated with the potential she saw in herself, and her life, Rats felt it as a criticism of herself. The strain and stresses were beginning to crack again. Rats decided one Thursday night that she would rather spend the weekend alone instead of spending Saturday night and Sunday with Helen. She was mortified to find Helen relieved by this as it meant she could take part in a massive canvass of their local housing estate.

By Friday evening Rats was brooding over Helen's casual acceptance of their broken date. Her mood worsened on Saturday morning when she received a notice to quit from her landlords. It threw her into a panic; she decided to have it out with them, but arriving at their office, found they were closed.

As she took the bus home she wrestled with two hurts. The first was the relief in Helen's face when she suggested not meeting over the weekend. She kept down the nagging, critical voice in her head that asked why, if she had really wanted to see Helen, was she playing games. Pretending she didn't want a thing just so she could be persuaded to have it. Testing Helen out? Her second hurt was why Helen, who so clearly wanted to take part in the weekend's activities, had not felt able to tell Rats so. This time, the small critical voice had full rein. Because you wouldn't have let her, it said, you'd have made her feel bad for suggesting it, worse if she actually did it. She knew you would have made a scene, that's why she kept quiet, she knew you would have sulked off, silent. Retreating into yourself, refusing to talk about it.

By the evening, Rats was in a bitter, angry mood. Angry at herself, angry at Helen. She felt they had reached another ending. Helen had her new life, her friends. She stayed with Rats out of pity and a sense of duty. Well, Rats needed no one's pity, least of all Helen's. She felt like getting drunk, very drunk. She went out, intending to buy beer and whiskey to bring back and drink in solitary indignation. But as she walked towards the off licence, she heard the sounds of jazz, a long note held and played with by a saxophone. She decided to drink in public and walked into the pub. Her determined look and walk made those men who casually looked her over, as they looked over all the women entering that bar, look away.

She ordered a pint and took it over to an empty table. The bar was fairly quiet, the trio played on. They were all elderly, all West Indian, a drummer, a keyboards player and the singer and saxophonist. A faded, hand-written sign proclaimed them as the 'Cyril Garner Trio'.

They played requests, slipping from 'Summertime' to 'Danny Boy' to 'Route 66' with an enviable ease. Most of the audience were indifferent to the performance. Rats took them all in, her gaze firm and uninviting. There was a table, mostly women who looked like teachers or social workers, there for the music. The pub's regular clientele held them at a distance although some men repeatedly came to the table, asking them to dance. They were not encouraged.

At another table were two boys, both maybe twenty, who sat looking nervous. One, wearing a fancy shirt and trilby hat, kept smoothing his hands on his trousers as if wiping sweat away. The source of his nerves was soon apparent when the saxophonist handed the microphone over to a middle-aged Irishman who sang a fair rendition of 'My Way'. He then offered the floor to singers. The least nervous of the two boys urged his friend forward. He took the floor and the microphone. He sang as if still before the mirror he must practise in front of, miming his routine. Rats expected his repertoire to be modern, pop music, but the tune he sang was older than she was. She couldn't place it, a run of the mill, crooner tune. By the second song his nerves were evident in his voice, which wavered and almost missed the notes. Rats noticed that the teachers were bored, taking the opportunity to refill their glasses. This wasn't what they had come for.

When the boy finished, Rats clapped him for his courage and his nervousness as much as for his music and wondered on the contentment of a life that found its major trial on the open floor of the local pub. But she wasn't one to grudge him his trials and pleasures. There was a break, the band adjusted their instruments, smoked cigarettes and drank the beers brought over by the glasses' man. Rats went to the bar again. When she returned to her seat she took in the rest of the pub. It was more crowded now and Rats realised that with the exception of herself, the teachers and the band, everyone in the pub was drunk. Not mildly drunk, but dead drunk. So drunk they could not stand or walk unaided.

She watched a woman, who may have been in her thirties, guide another, maybe in her fifties, to the toilet. They were as drunk as each other and bumped their way across the short distance from their seats to the toilet. When the woman came back her dress was caught up in her tights. Back at the table, the younger woman had to put the glass into her hand. There was a tenderness about these acts, quite out of keeping with the scenes around them. The women, she realised, had been coming in and out of the pub all night, at regular intervals with different men. All working men, all drunk and desperate. She knew there was an alley alongside the pub and guessed that in its darkness money changed hands, clothing was roughly pulled apart and bodies were traded. Looking around her at the men, she had some sympathy with the women's desire for oblivion.

The younger woman was singing now, starting ballads as she swayed in front of the empty bandstand, letting them fade tunelessly as she forgot the words. The band took up its position. The drunken woman was lurched into a parody of a waltz by a tall man, lumbering, almost as incapable through drink as she was. The band, playful, teased a waltz between the jazz rhythms. The pub carried on drinking, seething with the weight of the week's work being sloughed off. Rats had to brush off the unwanted attentions of various men. They seemed to be doing it out of habit, allowing themselves to be sharply and quickly dismissed.

Two tables down from her were a couple, their children and some friends. They had been smiling, intermittently, throughout the evening and, as Rats was at the bar for her third drink, the woman came and asked if she would join them. Rats' early evening mood of indignant anger at herself and Helen had mellowed. She was glad of the company and moved herself to their table. The music was flowing hot and sweet as she was introduced. She didn't retain all their names but was glad to be included. She chatted to the woman about where they lived and worked and the music. Good, the music, was their opinion and Rats marvelled out loud at the elderly dapper man fronting the line up, at ease with all the traditions of popular music and sentiments of the pub's clients.

Rats was drunk now, pleasantly so, and it didn't seem strange to her to think of the pub as a mass, a celebration of grace despite the women's comings and goings, the threatened fights, the air of violence contained, the desperate drinking and the maudlin mood induced by the Irish ballads, the Caribbean calypso, the American jazz. The gaiety, grim and dreadful as it might have looked to an outsider, settled on her like a benison. They were all singing along now, or tapping their feet to the beat.

Rats, carried away on this wave of well-being, accepted a drink from Rosallene's husband. She was shocked to recognise the man talking to the glasses man. He must have come in through the side door. While she was staring at him, Rosallene tapped her arm.

131

'All right love? You've gone as white as a sheet, not good for you, all that beer.' She called out towards the bar, 'Frank, get a whiskey for our friend.' She turned back to Rats. 'That'll settle you.'

Rats smiled into her concerned face. 'I'm okay, sorry. That man over there . . . '

'Declan?'

'Declan?'

'Glasses man, Declan.'

'No, the man with him.'

'Oh, I don't know him, do you?'

'Not exactly. But I need to talk to him.' Rats got up, was walking towards the bar as she spoke.

Declan was a short fellow with a limp. His face had the immobility associated with habitual over-indulgence of drink, or heavy use of sedative drugs. He seemed, to the casual observer, slow and dim-witted. But in the pub he reigned supreme. His evenings were spent shuffling from table to table, collecting glasses. For this he received payment in kind, in beer. In a pub like this it was important not to have too many empty glasses lined up. He also fetched drinks for the women when they were too drunk to walk to the bar and back. His main work, though, was to manage the conflicts and arguments in the pub, a keeper. He was never still. Even when he stood by the central pillar drinking his guinness, his eyes were constantly moving, his nerves anticipating, ready to deal with any trouble. Already tonight, Rats had seen him escort the dancer from the pub as gently as if he had been a baby, not a six foot blind drunk, fighting man.

The dancer, after his time with the woman, had pestered the women at the teachers' table. Then he had moved to Rosallene's table where he had been cheerfully dismissed, to stagger, solitary and out of time with the music, to his own rhythm. Declan had anticipated the exact moment his mood would slip from dancing to fighting. He had stood, a bear of a man, in the middle of the room, 'Where's ma drink? Who's had ma drink?'

He stopped and swayed, came to a standstill facing a table at which three young West Indians, sharply dressed, sat over their pils. 'Which of you . . .'

Before the tirade began, Declan barely reaching to the man's elbow, was beside him. 'Bedtime, boy. Come along now.' And surprisingly, the huge man lolloped along beside him and stood, almost bashful, as Declan put his hat into his hand and led him to the side door.

As Rats came up to Declan, he was weighing her up. Rats looked away from him to the man beside him. A man you would have taken for a tramp, from his clothing and his carriage, but whose face and hands were scrubbed clean as a baby. His eyes, Rats noticed, were blue-grey. She smiled at him. 'Hello, remember me?'

The man stood silent, Declan to one side watched them both. The music jumped and jived.

'You girl? Don't know you.'

'You do.'

'No girl, someone else. I don't know nobody. Not me girl.'

He stood before her, seeming to shrink into himself. Declan demanded, 'What's he to you? What's he done?'

'Nothing, it's nothing he's done. I've nothing against him. I want to talk with him about something private.'

The men looked at her, puzzled. Rats looked back at them, conscious she was drunk, but knowing this was her tramp. 'What's your name?'

'No name, girl. Leave me alone, now, there's a good girl.'

Rats felt Declan's hand on her arm. She looked over to where Rosallene sat, saw her puzzled face, conscious of the strange sight she must be making. She beckoned Rats back to her seat. Rats turned back to the man. 'Please, you can help me. I need your help.'

The eyes looked at her, not hostile, not blank, simply looked. At her, and through her. Declan's hand on her arm increased its pressure. As she went back to her seat the bell for last orders rang and the trio launched into their final number. Rats picked up the whiskey in front of her and raised her glass to Frank and Rosallene.

'Who's he then? Gave you a right turn.'

'I don't know who he is, he saw something I want to know more about. It involved me, I want to know what he saw.'

'A witness, is he?' Rosallene's face lost its smile, stiffened. 'Who are you then, you're not . . .'

'No,' Rats smiled. 'Do I look the part? I'm not tall enough. It was one night, walking home. Something happened to me. He saw it. I wanted to know exactly what he saw.'

Rosallen's face turned sympathetic; she reached for Rats' hand in a clumsy gesture of friendliness. 'Oh you poor love, I'll speak to Declan.'

Later, as the pub was emptying, Rosallene took Declan on one side. She came back to where Rats was sitting. 'Declan's not too keen to talk. But that man comes in here and the cafe across the road. He lives in the cemetery and on a doorstep, one of those disused houses on Manor Road. He's been around for years. I told Declan why you wanted to talk to him, but you know men.'

Frank interrupted them, wanting to know if they were staying back. Rats was tempted but took her leave of them, promising to look in again, probably next Friday night.

24

It was raining when Rats came out of the pub. As she walked home she experienced a feeling of *déjà vu*, of having been there before. She told herself that of course it was familiar, she walked this route near enough every day. But as she turned into her road, the feeling almost overwhelmed her and she knew herself to be in the emotional atmosphere of that night in January. There was the same music from the Bronx, the beat pounding out; the smell of fried chicken on the air and she almost expected to see the green Rolls Royce in amongst the cars double parked along the road.

There was no car, no body tonight, but the urgent fear of that night's walk home caused Rats' breath to come in short sharp intakes. She had a sensation of choking, but walked on, as anxious now as then to reach the security of her home. The fear helped her decide to go out tomorrow in search of the tramp. She would search and then she would give it up. She surprised herself, reaching the point where she could imagine giving it up, but having got there it was a strangely comforting place to be.

Rats slept that night, a heavy dreamless, alcoholic sleep. She woke at six, her mouth dry and her breath stale, staggered through the flat half asleep and made herself coffee.

She got up properly at ten, dressed and decided to set out. The cafe opposite to the pub was her first stop. She ordered tea and toast and sat down. It was fairly empty, just early morning shoppers in the main. She couldn't imagine the man mingling with this crowd. Perhaps he had been in earlier and gone. Rats finished her breakfast, was tempted to ask the serving woman whether she had seen him but was too shy and left with no more than a goodbye and a thank you.

A walk through the cemetery appealed. The calm she always felt there had been missing the few times she and Helen had searched it. It had become just so much ground to cover. Now, taking it at her own pace, the peace of the place descended on her. The paths were littered with a mass of brown and green fallen leaves. The trees were outlined, black in the grey wet sky. It could have been a frightening place, echoes of horror movies, nightmares in its edges; the trees standing guard, shrouding the dead, the long-mouldering bones and crumbling gravestones. But to Rats the stillness was a sanctuary; the sound of bird song, the rustle of small animals in the undergrowth and the constant renewal of life and death. She liked the idea of dead bodies rotting slowly into the earth, nourishing this profusion of growth.

Rats pondered on this and other things as she walked slowly along the paths. She was not aware of other people and found the isolation pleasant. It was as peaceful to find the man as not. Rats walked through to the furthest limits where the cemetery merged into the long gardens of the houses on Manor Road. The road curved and the gardens curved with it, radiating like a fan, giving an illusion of parkland stretching out for miles. She wondered whether there was a pathway across to the road but imagined there wouldn't be. She didn't relish the prospect of stumbling into someone's back garden. She retraced her steps back to the main entrance and on to the main road. There were a few shops on the right hand side, but mostly there were houses, four storey houses, some refurbished, others left to decay, some made into flats and bedsits, others left empty. The gardens were, on the whole, overgrown. Part way down, on the left, there was a house that flapped open, had run to seed. There was a pile of rubbish in the garden and scrubby bits of land that sustained ragged clumps of Michaelmas daisies. Rats inspected it closely, as she had all the empty houses along the road.

On the top step there was a construction of cardboard and rags. Rats looked more closely – there was a creature in there. She walked up the path. The pile on the doorstep remained still, but Rats made out a face, arms and feet. She recognised the face. It was the man. Rats met his look; it was as blank as it had been the night before in the pub.

'I've come back. Will you talk to me now?'

135

The man looked at her, didn't move, didn't speak to her. Rats stood where she was. 'Please, all you have to do is tell me. Nothing more, no involvement. Just tell me what you saw and I'll go away.'

He stirred, stretching his legs out, and spoke. 'Leave me be girl, I've nothing to tell you. Go away.'

'You know me, don't you?'

'Don't know you, girl. You don't know me. Seen you girl, seen you before, yes.'

'You know what I want to know, don't you? You know what it's about.'

'Not got a good memory, girl, too old. Don't remember much. Leave me now. I've nothing for you.'

Rats stood there, her hands in her pockets, wondering how much longer she could stand there, trying to persuade the man to talk. Her hand in her pocket closed on loose change and notes. 'Is it money? Will you talk to me if I give you money?'

The blank, not unfriendly face hardened. 'Pay your way for everything, you young ones. Buy and sell the world. I've no time for it, money. Keep it, see what it'll do for you.'

'I'm sorry if I offended you. I do need your help. Please tell me what happened that night.'

'Why girl? What's this thing to you?'

'You said you saw them, that night. I saw them too. I saw a man killed. I never knew what became of him, I never saw the death in the newspapers, nothing. It was as if it had never been.'

The man said nothing. Rats was uncomfortable, standing for so long. She pulled a milk crate over from the rubbish scattered over the garden and sat on it. 'It's a worry, seeing a dead body like that, it scared me. I tried to put it out of my mind but I couldn't, it haunted me. Then that car, the car I saw the body in. I saw it everywhere. It turned out to belong to the man who owned my firm. There were things going on in that firm, things I didn't understand. It was frightening, almost more than that body. I was followed, threatened. I don't know if I was in danger or not, I couldn't work out what was going on.'

'I seen you then, girl, didn't I? You were scared right enough.' The man started to laugh, a shrill, tinkling laugh. 'You were scared all right, scared of me, weren't you, girl? If you're going to be scared, pick the right one. Don't waste your time on things nothing to do with you.' The man wiped his eyes, he was smiling at her. 'What if I've something to tell you, say I told you. What then?'

'I only want to know, for myself.'

Rats felt he was on the verge of telling her and was terrified of doing something to make him stop.

'Well girl, I'll tell you. What did you see, then?'

'I saw a body, a man. I don't know what age he'd be, in the front seat of that car. He was dead, I think. Shot, I suppose, his head seemed ripped open at the back. His face looked almost normal.'

'What you thinking of now, girl, is how he got there. Didn't walk, did he? I saw them. There were four of them, in that alley runs alongside the railway. That alley opens out into wasteland, I was there. Back of those shops there's some cafes and restaurants. I was looking for throw outs and leave outs. Then I hear cars coming in and voices. I keep back in the shadows. My age, you learn to live quiet, keep out of the way. One of the men, he says what have you brought her for. I thought you wanted to see me. The woman she says he's crazy, crazy. Get away, he's got a gun. They were angry voices and scared. I was thinking, why were they there? Then I hear it, loud like an explosion and the woman screams and sobs. I hear her say "Why Cruze, why?" Then it goes muffled and I don't hear, only heavy breathing.'

'Did you say Cruze?'

'She did, the woman did.'

Rats felt sick, but excited. 'Then what happened?'

'These sounds, going on. It was strange, they seemed to know each other. Sometimes in places like this you get goings on, thieving and men going after women. But these, they were different. There was the sobbing and the man's voice, harsh, "You brought it on yourself". Then the noise again and it went quiet, the sobbing stopped.'

'Did you hear this or see it?'

'I didn't look, girl, not close. I could see the figures, standing. Then two on the floor. The men picked them up, wrapped them in something. The cars were started and driven off, they left the bodies there. I set off, down the alley, the other way.'

'That's not what I saw, though. It's horrible, but it's not what I saw.'

Rats felt confused, all her hopes had hung on this man. He should have had explanations, but all that had happened was a layer had been lifted off, revealing another set of problems, questions. One more grim story to weave into the fabric of London life. But he had said Cruze.

The man looked at her, seeming to sense her disappointment. 'Isn't finished, this story. I go down the alley, cross the road. There's a car parked, the car you saw, a man driving it . . . I go into the garages by the flat and turn to watch them. The man gets out, he goes down the alley. Two men come out, carrying something wrapped up. They get to the car and unwrap their package, it's the man. They put it into the car, as if it's a passenger, sitting up. Then they go back down the alley. Then I see you, girl. You come up and you stop and look. And then you run down to the phone, then you come back. The men are standing just outside the alley, waiting for you to pass. You come back, you don't look into the car this time. You just pass by. You walk past me, I see your face clearly then. I see the men looking at you, then you walk down the road.'

Rats shivered, she had felt watched that night, remembered clearly her sense of being followed. And she had been, had passed within touching distance of these strangers.

'The men watched you out of sight. Then they brought the second body out and put it into the back seat, like a passenger. Then they drove off. The windows of the car were shaded, they looked just like any car, a night out.'

'Where did they go?'

'I didn't go with them, girl. That's all I know, I've told you everything now.'

Rats sat thoughtful for a moment before she spoke. 'It's not what I expected to hear. It makes some things clear. Thank you.'

There was nothing more to say. Awkwardly she took her leave of him. As she walked back to her flat, her mind whirled. She had come closer than she had imagined to that death. Exactly how it all fitted together, she didn't understand. There was a pattern, she was sure, but something still evaded her. She couldn't make sense of the second body.

Rats was disappointed not to feel the elation she had anticipated. Back home, she wrote down the story and added it to the pile of information she and Helen had gathered. She sat for a while thinking things over, but nothing cleared for her. She wanted to talk with Helen, but still felt wounded. She was probably out, anyway, or if she was in the flat it would be crowded with friends from the campaign. Helen's friends. Rats would feel excluded, unable to tell her tale anyway.

It was time, too, that her mind was occupied by the notice to quit.

She was uncertain where she stood. The other people who had flats in the building she hardly ever saw. Rats could no more go and seek their advice than she could stand on the street corner and implore assistance from the people passing by. Through the evening her anxiety gathered. She wrote again to her landlords.

Dimly she thought that the landlords would need an official letter to get her out. Helen's friends could probably advise her, but she felt stubborn and proud. She would not go to them. She had little faith in her ability to stop the landlords. What they wanted, they would probably get. Anything she could do would be by way of delaying them. Rats let the housing problems recede. She thought about Helen, acknowledging how lucky it had been now she had not seen her this weekend. Remembering her relief in the summer when she realised Helen had come back to her, she felt guilty about her lack of faith in her. They had always had different priorities in their lives which had been a source of conflict in the past too, but also a source of strength. Rats, feeling the pressure of the death begin to slip away, resolved to be more patient, more trusting of Helen.

25

Later, Rats couldn't remember exactly when she saw the pattern come clear. It was sometime on the Sunday and she had to wait until Monday morning before she could finally prove it. She decided to tell Helen. She wanted to see her anyway, to talk to her about what she'd been thinking about them, her willingness to try and change. These last few months had been hard for them both and it seemed to Rats the death kept getting in the way, skewing their sense of each other. As the mystery of the death started to unravel, it cleared a space for herself and Helen. She was excited as she walked up to her estate.

There was a delay before the bell was answered. Just as Rats was on the point of going, she heard voices and then Helen opened the door to her, tousled and holding a dressing gown closed. She blushed when she saw her, the pinky red spreading down her neck and chest. Rats stood where she was, disconcerted. 'Have I interrupted something?'

Helen looked guilty, spoke too quickly. 'No, of course not. What would you be interrupting? Come in.'

A female voice echoed in the almost empty flat. 'Who is it? Bloody Jehovah's Witnesses? Get rid of them and come back here.' A pause, then the voice again, 'Helen?'

Rats stood where she was. 'I'm sorry I disturbed you. It wasn't important.' She turned away, walked back across the balcony to the stairs.

Helen came after her. 'Rats, wait. Don't go like that, please. Let me explain.' Helen caught hold of her. It was cold and she had no shoes on. Hopping from one foot to another, she asked Rats again to come in. Rats refused.

'I'll come round, later.'

'I won't be in later, don't bother.'

Helen stood for a moment, Rats turned and went down the steps. Humiliated.

Back at her flat, Rats' excitement at nearing the end of her search vanished. Touchy and over-sensitive as she was, she knew she had not misunderstood the scene she had stumbled into. She was shocked by Helen's deception, her own stupidity in not realising something had been going on. She wrote letters to Helen; bitter, angry letters full of recriminations and remorse. Letters she wouldn't send. And listened, wanting to go down and hear it was all a mistake as her doorbell rang on and off throughout the afternoon.

Monday morning found her back at the Reference Library looking up the Epping Forest suicides. She studied the pictures, but the man's features were still strange to her. She had the picture photocopied. She asked for and was brought copies of that same week's local London weeklies and the *Standard*. She scanned them all until she found that story. The *Standard* had different pictures, not the *Gazette*'s snapshots, but official photos, staid head and shoulders. There was something in this face – she looked at it more closely, closed her eyes and visualised the face in the car. It was hard to be absolutely sure. The bullet had ripped away the back of his head and death had fixed his features more firmly than this camera had. But there was something there, something horribly familiar. She read the accounts again. It was a love pact suicide, inexplicable to friends and relations alike. Rats read on, hoping to glean some more knowledge from the reports.

Leaving the library, Rats went in search of a phone box. She had to go through directory enquiries for the number. It was a short call, arranging a meeting for later that day. There was time to kill and she spent it idling around the shops. She bought a rattle and paper to wrap it in. Then she set out for Tottenham, consulting an *A to Z* in the newsagents to establish exactly where she was going.

Her arrival at Maureen's house was a flurry of greetings, parading the baby, filling the kettle, plumping up cushions. Rats was urged to make herself at home, hold the baby, come through to the kitchen. Her head was spinning but eventually she was settled on the sofa, a tray of tea and biscuits on the coffee table between them and the baby on Maureen's knee. Rats presented her with her rattle. The baby, with the habitual perverseness of her kind, discarded the toy in favour of the wrapping paper which she bundled into her mouth. Between the tea and the biscuits, the talk revolved around her. She had finally been called Catherine, after his mum, Frances after hers, then Gemma Marie. It seemed a huge name to saddle a small baby with, but she gurgled and grizzled contentedly enough.

Eventually, Rats moved on to the topic which brought her there. Maureen had kept off the subject of work, and Ralph, as if she knew the awkwardness there. Rats pulled out the photocopies; she had trimmed the words off, they were simply two faces.

'Maureen, do you know these two?'

She passed them across, receiving the baby in return. Maureen studied them. 'There's something familiar about the woman. The man I've never seen. Who are they?'

'They're people I'm interested in, not any special reason. I thought you might have known them.'

'You're a funny girl, aren't you. Where did you get these from? Ralph said . . . .'

Maureen stopped herself, but Rats encouraged her, saying there was no love lost between Ralph and herself. Maureen smiled, conspiratorially at her. 'Listen, it's what he said. You know I don't agree with him. I like you. Well, anyway, he said you were too nosey for your own good. That if you'd kept your nose out, as he put it, you'd still be in Pershing's good books and a job.'

'Oh well, I can't help it. I am curious, always have been.'

'I know love, women are. And no harm in it either. Men are so touchy, you'd think him and Pershing did have something to hide the way they go on. More tea?'

Rats accepted and went out to the kitchen to put more hot water on to the pot. When she came back Maureen said excitedly, 'Gerry, that woman. I know her.'

'Great, who is she?'

'It was thinking about Pershing. She was his great love. I knew I'd seen her somewhere, it was with him. He's a funny man, you know, been married a few times. Never keeps them, or his girlfriends either. He's always got a companion, but with that much money you can buy it, can't you? And good quality too.'

Rats nodded in what she hoped was an encouraging way.

'He met her, Susan, let me see, probably two or three years ago. They went about together, it was the big romance, you know. We expected them to get married. She's not been around for a long time though. The last time I saw her would be last Christmas, that's it. He took us all out for a huge meal, about eight of us, very generous he was, paid for it all, champagne, the lot.'

Maureen paused while she played through the scene again, 'It was lovely that night.' Her dreamlike trance was broken by a frown. 'Apart from the row. Fancy forgetting that. That was Pershing and Susan. He was a very jealous man, generous but he had to be in charge, you know. You had to appreciate what he was doing for you, if you understand what I mean, it was never just done. He and Susan had some sort of row, he was very rude, accusing her of all sorts. Sex. Called her a frigid bitch. She was angry with him, said he wouldn't know the difference, something like that. I hate it when people argue in public, there'd been something going on all night. I don't like people bringing sex into it like that.'

'How did it end?'

'It just sort of blew over. Someone said something, made a joke I think and then we were all talking about other things. He was possessive, she didn't like that. We used to talk together when they were carried away with their business talk, or in the ladies. A lot of secrets get shared there, don't they? She wasn't too keen on some of his work deals either. I can't remember exactly what it was, she did tell me, but I don't like to take too much notice of that side. I'll do my job and do it well, but I'd rather leave the other side of it to Ralph. Susan wasn't like that, though, she was in on everything.'

'Was she upset that night?'

'At the time, yes. She'd been humiliated. Men do that to women, put them down in public. But later, no, she was angry. She'd had enough, she said. I suppose she did leave him.'

'Interesting.'

'Is that what you wanted to know? Got designs on him yourself, have you? I wouldn't bother if I was you. You can do a lot better for yourself than that. Glamour and good looks are all very well, not to mention the bottomless wallet, but I wouldn't trust it myself. I'm happy with what I've got.'

'Me too,' said Rats, looking at her watch. 'I'd better be off, it's later than I thought, we've been nattering away for ages.'

'My God, her ladyship will be wanting a feed. It was nice to see you, Gerry,' Maureen said, rising from her chair. 'It really was. It's a bit of a strain sometimes, being at home all day. It'd be nice if you could drop by again. And we'll think of something more interesting to talk about than Pershing's love life, like our own.'

She gave Rats a broad grin and a nudge as she saw her out. Rats promised to call again. As she was closing the garden gate, Gemma Marie set up a wail. Jesus, it would drive me mad, she thought, hoping she could get to see Maureen again.

When she got back home, Helen was waiting outside for her. Rats had an impulse to simply ignore her, but she knew she couldn't carry it through.

'Rats, I've got to talk to you.'

'Come in then.'

Rats held the door open for Helen, locked it behind her and walked upstairs, barely acknowledging her presence. Inside she made tea without a word. Helen tried to cuddle her but was shrugged off.

'I'm sorry, I really am. It was a stupid thing to do, thoughtless and inconsiderate. I would have told you. I meant to say something sooner. Julie's been making it clear she was attracted to me for a while. I was flattered but not really interested.'

Rats raised her eyebrows.

'Well, maybe I was, yes. But I wanted to talk about it with you. You are my first consideration, even if it doesn't look like that. But lately, it's not seemed possible to talk to you; it's as if we can't really say what we mean anymore. And I am sorry, really sorry, you found out like that.'

The fury Rats had felt yesterday had gone. She believed Helen, but her disappointment and hurt were still there. Helen came over and kissed her, gently, until she responded to her, forgave her.

'It's all been too much lately. You moving out, Pershing, then this.

143

Sometimes I feel as if everything's out of control. And my landlord's hassling me.'

'You're better off without a landlord. Why don't you move into the flats? You could come in with me or have a place on your own. It looks as if we're going to win, you know, and if you're in when we do you'll get your tenancy agreed. We're the main item at the next housing committee and there's a lot of support.'

'I can't think about that now. I've got other things on my mind. I know now who it was who died. Pershing killed him.'

Helen sat back, surprised. Rats told her about meeting the tramp. 'The woman was Pershing's girlfriend. It must have been a jealous rage, Maureen said he was very possessive.'

'Not a rage, from what you told me. It sounds very well planned. It's not easy to fake suicide. Not spur of the moment stuff at all, most killing isn't, especially men killing women. It's just a useful plea for diminished responsibility or lenient sentencing.'

'Jealousy anyway. I went to see Maureen, she knew him. She said they were arguing last time she saw them together.'

'A dangerous emotion, jealousy.' Helen wagged her finger playfully in front of Rats. 'You want to watch out.'

'And you, too in that case,' said Rats, in the spirit of the exchange.

'It figures,' Helen continued, 'what I was uncovering was nothing very much. There's probably more to it, but I'm sure it's all the same sort of stuff, all just within the law. A man like Pershing doesn't need to break the law, he can buy it. And anyway, half the time it's there for the likes of him, to protect his interests in the first place.'

Rats made them fresh tea and told Helen what Maureen had told her about Pershing, his hostility towards Susan, his inability to form lasting relationships. Helen wondered whether he was repressing homosexual urges. Rats told here she thought that about everyone, and anyway, it wasn't about how much you disliked the opposite sex, was it?

'All the same,' Helen said, 'he doesn't come across as a man who liked women.'

'Do any of them? Hating women and femaleness seems to be part and parcel of being male. The poor sods can hardly help themselves.'

'Perhaps you're right. He sounds obsessed with women, all that jealousy. That is a sexual emotion. And taunting her sexually in public like that. Perhaps she was the one thing he couldn't control.'

'Probably. He could buy and sell pretty much everything else, and from what Maureen said he was used to buying women too. Susan must have been a challenge to him, with her independence attracting him and then clashing with him.'

'It's frightening to think about.'

'In what way?'

'That men still have the power. He couldn't control her and wanted to. But in the end it didn't really matter. He could just have her killed, and get away with it.'

'He's not got away with it though.'

'Well, yes. You, me and half a dozen other people know he killed her and the man, a boyfriend of hers I expect. But I don't suppose we can do much about it. To all intents and purposes he has got away with it. I don't imagine his conscience troubles him, he must have left that behind a long time ago. He sleeps easily enough on his exploitation of human need, death must be just another dimension.'

'We should do something. Try and get the case reopened by the police.'

'You wrote to the police before – didn't get you anywhere did it?'

'I didn't have any evidence then.'

'You don't have any now, only an accusation.'

The evening wore on. The issue of Pershing's crime could be taken no further by them. Rats mentioned her notice to quit, Helen urged her to visit various advice agencies. 'Go tomorrow, that place on the High Street, the green building has one on a Tuesday morning.'

Rats hesitated, part of her didn't really take it seriously. The part of her that knew all resistance was futile and that things were best left alone. Helen, sure that Rats would follow her advice, carried on talking about the campaign.

It was going well, there was a rumour that one of the national paper's leading investigative journalists was interested in doing a feature on Hackney. A number of documentary TV producers were sniffing around, likely to pick up either the racist bias in housing allocation or the plight of homeless families. The campaign group were pleased with themselves; those who had been in on the start of the project were seeing something like six years' work come to fruition. Success was not without its problems, however. With the increased publicity their group was in danger of being crowded out by the mainstream political activists and the professional community workers. It was a delicate stage in the group's history.

Helen was animated describing what they were doing and what

they planned to do next. She took it for granted that it was only a matter of time before Rats was fully part of the group. Rats could see that Helen had much to be proud of, but it was still off-putting to her. She understood the power relations instinctively. For Rats, knowing that power was knowing its effects on your life, its ability to structure and control, intimidate. To Helen it was a challenge. To know power was to know its weaknesses as well as its strength. Where it didn't control you as well as where it did. Helen saw the possibility of change. Rats saw only accommodation. It wasn't that they were growing apart. That would have been easy. They would just part, grieve, and in their new lives let the skin harden over old wounds. Here, though, they were striving to stay in touch, describe the new world for themselves, remain part of it for each other. They were both reluctant to give it up.

But over the next few weeks, the pressure began to make parting seem inevitable. Helen spent more and more of her time with the campaign. She had discovered a talent for managing the media, an ability to present their case sympathetically to often suspicious residents and a rare quality of being able to persuade the men with the cameras of their responsibility to the subjects of their films. She was in great demand, escorting the film crews on and off the council estates, smoothing their passage into everyone's life. Meanwhile, Rats retreated further and further into her stubborn self-reliance.

Helen had continued to see Julie. Helen was forcing her to face things too difficult for her. She cut off from it all. She avoided the campaign group, feeling herself a laughing stock, unable to believe Helen when she told her that almost all of them were involved with more than one person at a time. It seemed to Rats almost a point of principle with Helen that she have two lovers.

26

Rats was exhausted. As the year drew towards its close she found herself dwelling on the past. So much of that year had been a struggle with fear and uncertainty: the death, her job, Helen. What was left of them now – she had no job, she knew

146

how the man met his death, the ways Pershing was implicated in it, but it seemed a useless kind of knowledge. She had worked it out by chance and coincidence as much as anything, unwillingly. She hadn't ever really seen herself in the role of investigator. And at the end of it, what had changed? He was a powerful man, well connected and ruthless. She was scared of him, perhaps even more so now she knew rather than suspected his guilt. When she had wanted to know, she had imagined the knowledge would give her a lever on Pershing, give her the means and confidence to challenge him. It hadn't worked out like that at all.

The world seemed to contract. Once, the spaces had been filled with her fear; terrified as she had been, Rats now felt a sort of regret for it. There had been energy, even excitement in the terror. Now she could barely get herself up in the morning or remember her name. Nothing engaged her. Helen spent most of her time these days working for the campaign. Rats was interested, but far removed from it. She wondered what Helen saw in her, her own life seemed so full and rich, Rats couldn't imagine what she added to it.

Sometimes she wondered about joining Helen, getting involved, moving out of the flat. She was frightened that she had nothing to contribute, that it would not sustain her as it did Helen. She went along to a party they had, nervous of standing out, being ignored. She met Julie for the first time, determined to dislike her. As the evening wore on she was surprised to find herself unbending, laughing at her jokes, her outrageousness. Later, as they attempted to clear up, finally abandoning the task for coffee, Rats found herself alone with Julie. She made for the door, Julie put her arm out to stop her, casually. 'Don't go, I'd like to talk to you.'

Rats stopped, looked at her feet, the wall, anywhere but at Julie, smiling at her. It enraged her, the woman's calm assumption that she would want to speak to her. Rats thought she was mocking her. She saw in Julie everything she wasn't. The drink and the tiredness overwhelmed her, the more she tried to hold back the tears, the faster they fell.

Julie took her by the hand and led her to a settee, found cigarettes and a forgotten can of beer. 'I'm not doing this to hurt you, you know. I'd like us all to be able to get on, do things together. I'd like to get to know you as well. It doesn't have to divide us.'

Rats dragged on her cigarette a few times. 'I don't count anymore, it's you and her now. This is all part of it, I don't fit in. I'm just a left over, second best.'

'It must feel like that, like a rejection, but it isn't. You must know Helen's feelings for you. You two have something I'll never have. Helen thinks the world of you, there's no way she's going to give you up. There's no reason why she should.'

'Don't you want her to? What do you want? You're just being kind. You can afford to, because you're number one now. Anything we had is in the past, finished. Like that, used up, useless.'

Rats held her cigarette up, ash lengthened along it. She reached around for an ashtray, stubbed out the cigarette and stood up, with the clumsy dignity of the very drunk.

Before Julie could reply, the door opened and Helen and the others came in. She looked questioningly at Rats, then at Julie. Rats moved unsteadily towards the door, the others let her pass, Helen pulled her back, turning her face to hers. 'Where are you going? Have some coffee.'

Rats struggled with her. 'Let me go, let go of me.' She was shaking with tears, with anger. The atmosphere in the room hovered between tolerance and annoyance. Sandra, whose flat they were in, wished they would all go home. She found emotional scenes distasteful, especially at this hour of the morning.

Helen walked out of the room, her arms around Rats. Julie got up and followed them. There was the sound of voices, doors closing, footsteps along the balcony. Out on the estate, the three of them walked, Rats supported between Helen and Julie. The cold air had not sobered her up; if anything she seemed drunker now than before. As they walked, she protested. 'I don't know why you don't just leave me. Go off together, it's what you want to do. Let me sit down, I'm tired. I'm so tired. Let me go.' And between times she sobbed, great gulping sounds that shook her body. Julie and Helen soothed and cajoled her, concentrating on keeping her upright. They all went back to Helen's flat and Julie made some coffee while Helen put Rats to bed.

In the living room Julie and Helen talked in whispers about what to do, serious concern on their faces, like the parents of a recalcitrant child.

'It wasn't the best time to talk to her, I know. But I couldn't stand the way she just pretended I didn't exist all night. I had to say something.'

'She wasn't ignoring you. She even said to me at one point she could see the attraction.'

Helen played with the spikey tendrils at the back of Julie's head.

'And she meant it. She's trying, but it's not easy for her.'

Julie shrugged off Helen's hand and lit a cigarette. 'I can't believe this hasn't happened before.'

Helen sighed, turning away from her. 'Not like this it hasn't. It's different here; the talking and trying to do things differently. She's not used to it. Neither am I, it's just I've more to gain from trying to get it right.'

Julie stood up to go, put on her jacket. 'Nothing's easy in this life, kid.'

Helen got up as well, held her briefly, 'Come by tomorrow, will you? I'll talk to her.'

In the bedroom, Rats was still awake. As Helen came in, kicking her shoes off, she began to apologise. Helen shushed her gently. Later Rats was very sick, then slept. Helen lay awake beside her, thinking.

The next day, and for days after Helen and Rats talked, Helen and Julie talked, and finally the three of them together in a pub acknowledged their place in each other's lives. During this period, Rats spent a lot of time with Brenda, talking to her about Helen and Julie. At first she had been angry that Brenda challenged her, was prepared to accept how upset Rats was, but constantly pushed at her to see Helen and Julie's point of view.

Gradually, though, Rats would take from Brenda arguments and questions she couldn't from Helen. She began to see things less as her failure and more as a challenge with possibilities and advantages. The changes wouldn't happen overnight, they wouldn't always be straightforward, but Rats felt better about herself, beginning to take charge. She no longer felt at the mercy of the world.

However, the slow building up of her confidence took a knock. Her letter asking the landlord to withdraw the notice to quit was firmly refused. He wanted the flat for his daughter who was returning from abroad after Christmas. He gave her two weeks to be out.

Rats reacted by shutting off, trying to pretend it wouldn't happen. She wanted to tell Helen, but never could. Helen was immersed in the squatters' campaign. Victory was almost assured and they were all working flat out, trying to get the council decision through before Christmas. Finally, their success forced it out of her. The jubilation in the council chamber spilling out on to the streets, playing like children in the snow as they trailed the good news back with them brought the reality of her own situation home to her. That night she told Helen. Winning their fight elated her, she was fearless, 'He can't do it. He's got to get a court order. Write and tell him. And move, come here. The place is a dump anyway.'

Rats wrote the letter, hoping it would be the end of it and thought about moving. A new start for the new year. The idea appealed.

A Christmas card from Maureen stirred her guiltily into visiting. As she sat hazy from sherry and mince pies in the splendour of Gemma Marie's first Christmas, she remembered her last visit, the relief of fitting together the pieces in the puzzle of Pershing's guilt. Coming home, she dwelled on it, turning over again the conversations with Helen, her insistence that they could take it no further, had no tangible evidence to warrant going to the police.

That evening she was going out with Helen. As she was getting changed, there was a knock at the door. Rats hurried into her clothes, alarmed. The knocking persisted. A key turned in the lock. She stood face to face with her landlord and his agent, Matthews. 'What do you think you're doing? Coming in here like this.'

Ignoring her, they came in. The agent had a clip board and began walking around checking things off a list. Rats was furious. 'Just what the hell do you want? This is my flat; you can't just barge in like this.'

The landlord pulled up a chair for her, 'Sit down, Miss Flannagan. I want a word with you about my flat.'

The agent paused in his task and handed a wad of papers over to him. 'It's some months now since you paid the full rent, you are in arrears and don't appear to have taken any notice of my letters to you. You have terminated your tenancy. I'm repossessing the flat.'

'You must be joking. You can't do this.'

The landlord stood up, spoke to his agent, 'Get rid of this junk will you, now.'

He came towards her, Matthews hovering in the background. 'Move, woman.'

Rats flinched as he thrust forward at her. She was hardly able to believe what was happening around her. Matthews was pulling her posters off the wall, her books from the shelves, heaping them on the floor. She followed him helplessly into the bedroom as he emptied drawers out on to her bed.

The landlord pulled her back. 'I'm beginning to lose my patience. I want you out tonight and no messing. You've had fair warning.'

At that moment, Helen appeared in the doorway, a worried look on her face. From the bedroom came the sound of Matthews' rifling

Rats' belongings. Rats started to speak; she hadn't got far before Helen took charge. 'You are acting illegally. If you don't leave at once, I will and I'll be back with the police. You have no right to come in here like this and no excuse for behaving in this way.'

Her tone was assured, her look fierce. They didn't doubt her capability.

'You don't understand. This woman owes rent for months, has neglected the flat, has behaved irresponsibly. I'm only protecting my interests.' He came towards her, his voice full of the reasonableness of what he was saying.

Helen was unmoved. 'Forget it, call off your thug in there and get out.'

The landlord hesitated, then he called out to Matthews who joined him in the living room. Standing on his dignity, he turned back to face them from the doorway. 'You haven't heard the last of this. I'm the one who'll be going to the police. Don't think you can get away with this. I'll be back.'

Rats and Helen listened in silence to their footsteps down the stairs, the slamming of the front door and the car engine revved noisily down the street. Then they both started to laugh, hugging each other. Whenever they tried to speak, a new wave of hysteria silenced them. Finally, wiping the tears from her eyes, Rats said, 'You were magnificent, wonderful. I don't know what I'd have done on my own, I was scared rigid. They just took me by surprise.'

Helen made a mock bow, 'All in the line of duty, Ma'am.'

Then she continued, 'But I can't guarantee to do it again. You're going to have to go. He's going to get you out, one way or another. You might as well leave on your own terms.'

Dusty emerged from his hiding place under the bed, 'He's hardly going to protect you, is he? Here, pusscat, come to your mother.'

The cat shook himself and wandered over to them, rubbing nervously around their legs. Rats picked him up, 'I've been thinking anyway. I want to come and live with you. We both do, don't we, puss?'

Puss purred contentedly, squeezed between them.

They didn't go out that night, instead they started to pack. Helen spent the night there just in case the landlord came back. The next day, Helen went off to try and arrange a van, leaving Rats to continue packing. Rats was in a ruthless mood as she worked, throwing away

151

almost as much as she decided to keep. She picked up the dusty pile of papers from their investigation into Pershing. She was tempted to discard that too. But it wasn't as easy as that to rid herself of it.

She sat down, looking through them again. It seemed plausible enough to her. She tried to imagine taking them into the police station. She still couldn't see herself doing that. But it irked her, to think of him getting away with it. Leaving the papers to one side she returned to her sifting and sorting.

Helen returned with a van and people to help. They worked well together. Rats was shy at first, she barely knew them and was overwhelmed by their openness and willingness to help her. Helen retold the story of the landlord's visit, playing up Rats' heroism. The women praised her courage and Rats was embarrassed.

As the last load was packed, Rats took a final look round. The papers were still there; she picked them up before leaving.

27

The seasonal post that year was swelled by one more plain paper envelope. Rats had finally written her letter, outlining the facts as she knew them and sent it to the police.

It had a credible ring to it that made the officer reading it check the contents against their records. He established a similar report had come in some months previously on which no further action had been taken. He was tempted to let it go as the work of an oddball, but he was bored, there was little for him to do that day but catch up on his backlog of court reports. Anything that would delay that further was welcome. He checked the suicide, found it had happened as described in the letter. Although he knew that the information could have come from the newspapers, he was intrigued.

He went back to the area reports for the night in quesion. It was the usual catalogue of Road Traffic Offences, Drunk and Disorderlies, Petty Thieving, then something caught his attention. The beat constable had filed a small item; evidence of assault in the wasteland running between the railway and the parade of shops on Stamford Hill. Blood on the wall and on a man's scarf. He had investigated, but found nothing. There had been no complaints about a disturbance.

Looking at his watch, the officer decided it wasn't worth starting on the reports now. His shift was almost finished, a few drinks with the lads then off on leave. He phoned through to CID. 'A Christmas present for you all,' he said, smiling at his own joke with the satisfaction of knowing he was interrupting their Christmas party. Against its background noises, he arranged for the letter to be collected, putting it into an envelope marked 'For Action. Urgent.'